The Secret of the
STONE CIRCLE

The Secret of the
STONE CIRCLE

JUDITH SILVERTHORNE

Edited by Barbara Sapergia
Cover image: Aikey Brae photo copyright Allan Akers 2009 www.allanakers.com
Interior Illustration by Neil Jones
Cover design by Jamie Olson

Library and Archives Canada Cataloguing in Publication

Silverthorne, Judith, 1953-
        The secret of the stone circle / Judith Silverthorne.

(From many peoples)
ISBN 978-1-55050-431-6

        I. Title. II. Series: From many peoples

PS8587.I2763S435 2010   jC813'.54   C2010-900426-4

COTEAU
BOOKS
2517 Victoria Avenue
Regina, Saskatchewan
Canada   S4P 0T2
www.coteaubooks.com

Available in Canada from:
Publishers Group Canada
9050 Shaughnessy Street
Vancouver, British Columbia
Canada   V6P 6E5

Available in the US from:
Orca Book Publishers
www.orcabook.com
1-800-210-5277

10 9 8 7 6 5 4 3 2 1

Coteau Books gratefully acknowledges the financial support of its publishing program by: the Saskatchewan Arts Board, the Canada Council for the Arts, the Government of Canada through the Canada Book Fund, the Government of Saskatchewan through the Creative Economy Entrepreneurial Fund, the Association for the Export of Canadian Books and the City of Regina Arts Commission.

*For my mom, Elaine Iles; my sister, Darlene Ellis;
my two grandmothers, Elizabeth Assman and Mary Iles;
and all our ancestors in our family circle of women.*

*And to Kay Parley, a fine and true Scotswoman,
also from my family circle of women and my personal
inspiration in all that she does, knows and shares.*

EMILY'S MAP – the way to Aikey Brae

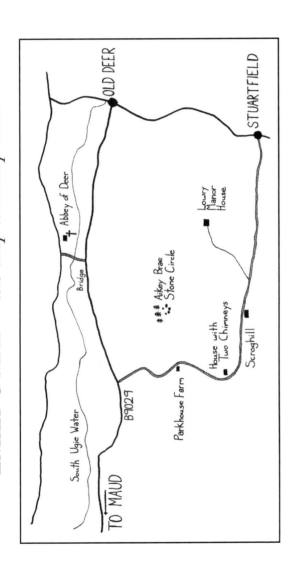

CHAPTER ONE

Emily crunched the last sweater into her suitcase and jammed the lid down. Holding it shut with one knee, she pulled the zipper closed, tucked her journal into a secure pocket of her backpack and flopped onto the bed.

"Did you pack your green sweater?" Kate asked, entering the attic bedroom.

"I have plenty of warm clothes," Emily answered her mom. "You know it's summertime in Scotland, too."

"Maybe, but the weather could be chilly and damp. The wind blows right off the North Sea. And didn't your dad say you might go to the Highlands as well? There could be snow in the mountains."

"No, I'm not taking a parka," Emily said, anticipating her mom's next suggestion. "I packed my bathing suit, though." She laughed, and jumped up to stand by her mom. She was surprised to find that she'd grown during the summer. Now she could look straight into her mother's eyes.

Kate gave a little sniff. "I doubt you'll need it."

Emily saw worry in Kate's eyes, and realized that her mom was more anxious about her going away – and going with her dad – than concerned about what she'd packed.

Emily gave her a quick hug. "I'll be fine Kate."

"I know Em." Kate grinned at Emily's use of her first name. "But remember, I'm still 'mom' to you."

"Okay, Mom." Besides her dad, Kate was the only person who called her Em, and she wouldn't see her for two weeks. Unexpectedly, Emily felt the flurry of but-terflies doing somersaults in her stomach. She wasn't sure how she'd feel, seeing her dad, David, for the first time since her parents had decided several months ago to get a divorce. She wanted to see him, but was afraid he might be forgetting her. She wondered if she'd still know how to talk to him.

He'd be working part of the time, heading a team on some geology dig in the rift valley of the Central Lowlands, and giving a lecture at a scientific conference. But first, they were going to have a week for sightseeing.

She was a little nervous, too, about flying and taking her first trip out of North America. She could hardly imagine travelling for the more than eleven hours it would take to get to Edinburgh.

Kate gathered Emily's discarded clothes and headed

downstairs, calling over her shoulder, "Come down soon; it's almost time to leave."

"Okay," she answered, imagining the famous places she and her father would visit. She'd been studying them on the Internet. Mist creeping over Loch Ness and the first rays of sun reflecting off the high peaks of Ben Nevis. To start with, they'd be staying at a cottage in the northeast county of Aberdeenshire, exploring the places where her ancestors came from. Places with odd names like Scroghill, Maud and Old Deer. Grandmother Renfrew had told her about them.

Her grandmother's family, the Elliotts, had lived in that area, in meagre homes, working as labourers on tiny plots of land. She wanted to see their houses – their *crofts,* as the Scots called them – where they'd struggled for generations to make a bare living.

She ran her fingers over the patchwork quilt on her bed, hand-stitched by her grandmother, using many-coloured scraps from clothing belonging to members of their family. It was like a family history she could see and touch every day. And now she was going to the place they'd all come from, to follow their story back in time. She felt almost afraid, but the touch of the old quilt anchored her in this narrow attic room in her grand-mother's house. For although Emily and her mother lived in the city, this place had always been what Emily meant when she said the word home.

It was hard to leave this room in the stone house

built by her great-grandfather, George Elliott, over a hundred years ago. When she came back, it might belong to others.

After her grandmother's death, all the farm equipment had been sold at auction. The farmland, now rented, would be sold in the fall. Emily and her mom would return to the city – unless she could convince her mom and aunts to keep the farm.

At the foot of her bed stood the old wooden trunk that crossed the ocean with her grandmother's family. A hand-braided rag rug warmed her feet. And she could almost see Grandmother Renfrew sitting in the carved-back rocking chair by the window.

Emily set it gently rocking and gazed out at the prairie. She and her grandmother used to walk through the grasslands, while Gran told her about the native plants and ways to use them for food and medicines. They'd take their lunch to the local landmark they called Sentinel Rock, where Emily first learned that she could do more than imagine the world of her settler ancestors – she could actually join them for a while in that long-ago time. She still didn't know how it was possible.

Emily felt a deep longing to be in the meadows one more time, but she had to leave soon for the city airport – over an hour away – and she knew Kate would call her at any moment. Emily tried harder these days to pay attention to the things that would help her mother not to worry so much about her, things like trying to be on time. And Kate, in turn, had accepted that her daughter was a very different person from herself, much less concerned with rules and schedules.

Emily picked up an old wooden box from the night table and opened the lid. Inside lay a small hand mirror with intricate filigree metalwork and inlaid stones on the frame and handle. She'd found it here in the stone house earlier in the summer, in a secret compartment under the hearth of the fireplace.

The mirror seemed to have been left for her to find.

Should she take it with her? No, that would be stupid. It could get lost or broken. She picked it up and felt the metal and glass warm in her hands.

She studied her face in the mirror, which was cloudy in spots after its long travels. Moments later her image wavered, as if light shifted inside the glass. Her face, her long brown hair, faded, and mist swirled across the glass. It cleared to reveal a circle of large stones on a grassy hill. Some stood upright, while others had fallen on their sides or lay partly buried in the earth, crusted with orange and lime-green lichen.

By one of the upright stones, she made out a human shape. The figure moved closer. For a moment everything blurred, and then a face filled the mirror, the face of a young woman with black hair loose to her shoulders and a roughly woven shawl over her head. Her dark eyes seemed to look right at Emily, as if she were no further away than the distance to the mirror.

Emily's hands trembled and her very bones felt cold. The woman needed to tell her something.

Bring it back.

Emily jerked and almost dropped the mirror. When she looked again, the image had dissolved.

Who was the woman, and how could she speak through the mirror?

Emily returned it to its box and began pulling things out of her backpack. Some could be stuffed into the outside pockets of her suitcase, but the mirror had to go wherever she went: it had to go in the backpack. As she finally settled everything back in her luggage, she was panting as if she'd run a race, but now everything felt right.

Now she could leave the stone house.

CHAPTER TWO

Emily stepped out of the rented cottage in the town of Maud, into a day of perfect blue sky. Bright sunshine defined each detail of the rambling Scottish village and the hollow in which it sat. Soft breeze rippled tall grasses in a strip of moorland bright with yarrow, bluebells and other wildflowers. Outside the village, rolling hills stretched as far as she could see. Except for the rocky peaks in the distance – *tors* was the local name for them – and the far-off calls of rooks, Emily could have been on the Canadian prairies. But her mom had been right. It was cool enough in the early morning to make her glad of the thick green sweater she'd pulled on over her T-shirt.

Emily could hardly believe she and her dad had arrived in Scotland only the day before. They'd met in Heathrow airport to catch their connecting flight to Edinburgh. She'd worried about their meeting, but he'd immediately drawn her into his strong arms and she'd held him tight.

After the hug, though, they looked at one another with unfamiliar awkwardness. She saw lines on his face that weren't there before, and he was thinner. He looked tired, and his straight dusty-blond hair hung unevenly over his shirt collar. He'd never used to let it grow that long.

They'd stood for a few moments at a loss for words, then hurried to catch their flight.

On the plane she tried to tell him about leaving the farm, but for most of the flight, he sat hunched over his laptop. He worked too much, just like Mom.

As they approached Edinburgh and she saw the outlines of its famous castle, Emily remembered coming through customs at Heathrow. The officer, a burly, unsmiling young man, had started going through her backpack as if he planned to examine every pen and notebook, and she'd felt a wave of fear that he'd see the mirror. What if he didn't believe it was hers? His fingers were almost touching the metalwork when an officer at the next counter, a woman, asked him about some regulation or other. After he answered, the burly man looked down at the backpack, a puzzled look on his face, and waved her through.

Emily couldn't remember when she'd felt so relieved. What if he'd tried to take the mirror away? She wanted to tell her dad about the mirror, but she didn't feel ready yet. Maybe when they were settled in the cottage. She hoped he'd understand how important it was to her.

At the Edinburgh airport, they rented a blue Ford Focus and drove to their rented cottage in Maud, too tired to do anything but sleep. The only thing she noted was that the houses had names instead of numbered addresses and that theirs was called Nicholls Cottage. At breakfast the next morning, David made oatmeal porridge, but he wasn't quite the dad she'd always known. He kept checking for e-mail and phone messages, as if he was trying to avoid talking to her.

She'd wanted to ask if he and Mom might get back together. Or what he thought would happen to her if they didn't. But he kept the topics light, and there was a sadness in his eyes. Maybe he didn't want to answer her questions.

At least he seemed enthused about going on a hike to see a few landmarks they'd chosen from the brochures their landlady had left, but he was sure taking his time getting ready. Emily set her backpack on the stone step. Her foot tapped an impatient beat. There were ruins of fortresses, castles and abbeys in the vicinity, and even more important, there were several stone circles. She wanted to see them all.

Her dad came out then, his camera equipment slung around his neck, an ordnance map in his hand. He'd explained that an ordnance map was a hiker's friend, showing every road, footpath and geographic detail and the elevations of every place of interest in the area.

"Ready for Aikey Brae?" he asked.

"You bet!" Emily grabbed her backpack from the step and her dad helped her settle the straps across her shoulders. Aikey Brae was the closest stone circle.

"Looks like we head west for about a mile and a half along the B9029 and then turn onto a minor road," he said, studying the map.

Emily peered over his shoulder. "Looks easy. Let's go."

She led the way single file along the road, which followed the contours of the landscape around and over the hills that led between Maud and the village of Old Deer. They spoke little, still shy with one another, although they did stop often to admire the landscape and take pictures. After a time, they turned south onto a narrower, winding road, up a gentle slope with fields on either side.

The countryside was so beautiful, the air so fresh and filled with the scent of flowers, that Emily found herself relaxing. She was walking on ground her ancestors had walked on. She was going to learn more about them.

"Okay, this is the third bend," Dad said, consulting the map as they came to an intersection with several lanes. All of them led into different parts of a farm called "Parkhouse," according to a large sign on the side of a building.

Emily noticed a smaller sign across the road, half-hidden by a hawthorn bush, with "Aikey Brae" hand-painted in faded letters and an arrow pointing to an overgrown track up a steep hillside. "I guess we go up this way," she said.

They followed the path, walking in the wheel ruts of some heavy vehicle. On either side, tall gorse hedges with masses of bright yellow flowers were offset by wild rose bushes and a mix of tall grasses and flowers that spread over low stone borders.

At the top, they had to make a choice: to continue on a path across the hillside, or to enter a fenced wooded area bordering an enclosed field.

"To the right, and then through those trees," said Dad, after studying the directions again. "We only need to go about two hundred metres."

One at a time, they passed through a kissing gate – a small rectangular enclosure with a hinged gate that moved to let them into the small space, and swung in the opposite direction to close the first opening and allow exit from the enclosure to the other side.

"Great to stop livestock from getting through," Emily commented, having figured out the purpose of the odd entryway.

As they followed the short path to the woods, sheep stared at them from the other side of the barbed-wire fence. At the edge of the copse, Emily paused for a moment, peering into tall spindly pines, so dense there was almost no undergrowth. The interior was eerie and dark, and she couldn't see through to the other side. Was this the right way to the stone circle?

As her eyes adjusted, Emily saw a vague opening into the thickly packed trees. "I guess we go through here."

Once they stepped inside, a path seemed to appear before them, though it vanished into darkness.

"I wonder which way we head?" Dad said.

Emily gave him a curious look. Couldn't he see there was only one obvious path?

She led him through the gloomy thicket, feeling sudden coolness. The carpet of needles underfoot muffled sounds. Sunken green-hued stones edged one side of the path, leading them forward like Hansel and Gretel's trail of crumbs. The ground, the trees and even the shadows had a strange green glow, as if Emily and her father had entered a magical emerald world. They fell silent, feeling peacefulness descend around them until they came to a bend that turned right.

A moment later, they stepped out of the trees into bright, shimmering sunlight.

In front of them lay a great circle of massive rocks, standing guard over a sweeping series of valleys. Five stones stood upright. The others lay on their sides in a tangle of grass, some partly buried so that it seemed the land was slowly taking them back. Patches of yellowy-orange and green lichen grew on the pitted rocks.

Emily shivered, even though she could feel the sun on her hair. The enormous rocks, their great age, and the incredible work it had taken to haul them here and place them in the circle took her breath away. She realized how important the stones must have been to the people who brought them here, for each had a strength and a presence that even she, who lived in such a different world, recognized.

More than that, these were the stones she'd seen in the mirror.

Dad walked over to one of the standing stones and examined it closely. He was almost six feet tall and the stone rose slightly above him.

"These embanking stones – they're the ones that anchor the structure – are local pink-and-grey granite. Those hard, dark, fine-grained rocks are whinstone, which seems unusual for the area," he said. All the other circle stones were plain grey. "Each of these must weigh several tonnes. It's amazing that they could haul these megaliths up here."

"Megaliths?" Emily gave her dad a puzzled look.

"It just means really big stones," he said. "*Mega* is for the really big part, and *lithos* is Greek for stone."

"Neat," said Emily. Having a geologist dad really came in handy sometimes.

She walked over to a pockmarked, elongated slab on the southern arc of the circle. One end was curved in a shape that reminded her of the prow of a ship.

Dad joined her. "That's called a recumbent stone. It's the one they would have used in their rituals. All these megalith structures were used for ritual purposes."

"What kind of rituals?" Emily asked, imagining sacrifices of lambs, or worse. She felt chilled even though she had warm layers of clothing on.

"Probably seasonal – to welcome spring and the renewal of life, and in the fall to celebrate a bountiful harvest. They'd have probably used grains, water and other symbolic articles for offerings," he reassured her. "And maybe they did some burial ceremonies."

As Dad inspected the stone, a gentle mist appeared. Emily moved around the outside of the circle, and the mist turned to light fog. She thought she could see people moving among the stones as they chanted and prayed.

The wreath of haze thickened and Emily lost sight of her dad, though she still heard the click of his camera shutter at intervals. She could also just make out the curve of the closest standing stone.

And was that a shape against the stone?

The fog shifted, and Emily saw a young woman in a dark ankle-length shift, clutching a tattered shawl over her head, half-concealing her face. She seemed to be watching Emily.

Everything went deafeningly silent as the fog closed around the woman. She looked so alone. As she moved her head, the shawl slipped, revealing long black hair hanging raggedly past her shoulders, and dark eyes that seemed to ask a question.

It was the woman from the mirror! Instinctively, Emily stepped towards her.

The fog vanished and Emily stood on a hill, barren except for the standing stones – all of them upright now! She could see clearly in all directions – and there were no farms or animals in sight, only occasional bushes or small stands of trees on the hillsides and in the valleys.

Startled, she looked around for the woman, who had somehow moved behind her. In a moment the two of them were again shrouded in fog. The stranger stood very close, her eyes wild and imploring. Emily reached out to touch her.

Instantly, the image disappeared and the fog dissolved.

What had just happened? Was Emily's imagination playing tricks because Dad had talked of burials? She couldn't believe that; the images had been too real. The landscape had certainly changed – though now it was back to normal – and the woman's clothing was definitely from another time.

Emily was glad she'd brought the mirror with her. She'd try looking into it when they got back to the cottage.

For now, she gazed at the stones, wondering about the woman in the mist. Who was she? Had she lost

someone dear? Somehow, her distress seemed more pro-
found. And there was more than sorrow in the woman's
eyes, there was anger.

"Ready to head off?"

"Aaagh!" Emily yelped.

"Why so nervous?" Dad asked, stepping over to her.

"I didn't hear you coming." She took a quick breath.

"I'll make more noise next time." He chuckled.

After a moment, Emily asked, "Didn't you think that
fog was really weird?"

"It was just a little mist," Dad said, putting the cap on
his camera lens.

"But I couldn't see you across the circle."

"Are you sure you're okay, Emily?" He frowned,
looking at her. "I could see you perfectly fine."

"I must have been imaginings things." She patted his
arm. "I'm okay."

"Good." He raised his camera to take a shot of several cottages nestled in the valleys below, all within easy
walking distance of one another.

"Everything is so close here, isn't it?" Emily said. "Not
like back home where you have to go quite a few kilo-
metres before you come to a town or even another farm."

"It wasn't always that way in Canada. When the set-
tlers first came to the prairies, there was someone on
every quarter section."

"Yes, I know," said Emily, having seen it for herself.
"The farms were all laid out in square grids. Here they

seem to be plunked anywhere and everywhere in all shapes and sizes."

They gazed out over the collage of irregular-sized farms amid fields scattered over the curves of the hills. Gorse hedges or low stone walls bordered each of them, reminding her of Grandma Renfrew's "crazy" patchwork quilt with its random shapes and colours.

Dad tucked his camera away. "Dare I ask where we're off to next?"

"You might like to try the Abbey of Deer," boomed a gruff Scottish voice from the edge of the trees.

Emily and Dad whirled around to find a big hulk of a man plodding across the field. He had a thick grey beard and his disarrayed whitish hair was crammed under a tam. A well-worn kilt swished around his thick, hairy legs. Emily had to stifle a laugh. She hadn't expected to see a man wearing a kilt for everyday in the middle of the countryside. And he was no romantic hero, no Rob Roy or William Wallace, just a determined looking middle-aged guy who obviously loved giving information.

"Murdoch Lowry, ready to be of service," he said, reaching out to shake their hands. Only "Murdoch" came out more like "Mairrrrdohhch." The guy could really roll his "rrrs." "I see you've been admiring our ancient site."

They introduced themselves and Dad asked, "Are we on your land, then?"

"Nae, though it used to be on private land. Of course anyone can walk almost anywhere these days according to the new Scottish laws. The owner's a grand chap to have preserved the place and fenced in the area to allow the public to stroll about without worrying about bulls in the fields and such."

"It's a fascinating place," said Emily. "Do you know any of its history?"

"Aye, it's said that there was once a Pictish village nearby to the north, but little is known about the origins of the standing stones, except that they are probably about four thousand years old. The grove of trees behind you was planted less than a hundred years ago, so before that one could have seen great distances in every direction."

Emily glanced around, remembering the vision she'd seen in the mist. The woman had to have lived before the planting of the trees, then. But how far before? And how long had it taken the stones to sink?

Murdoch Lowry continued. "The area is more famous from the 1300s, when Robert the Bruce's brother, Edward Bruce, killed the Earl of Buchan, who was to have become King of Scotland. Bruce waged a vicious campaign against the Buchans, and the final battle was fought on the steep slope on the other side of these trees. The Battle of Aikey Brae is said to have been so brutal that only twelve warriors were left standing!"

Could the woman in the mirror have come from that period? Maybe she'd lost someone in the battle. But it had happened over seven hundred years ago. How could she be seeing someone from that time? Surely her mirror wasn't that old. Even as she finished the thought, Emily shivered and realized that it could be.

She had to get back right away and examine the mirror! She needed to find out why this woman had come to her and what she wanted.

CHAPTER THREE

With an effort, Emily brought her attention back to the present. Murdoch Lowry and David were heading back through the trees. Emily sighed and followed them. She might as well learn what she could. Maybe seeing the battle site would give her clues about the woman from the past.

Once they reached the edge of the pine woods and passed back through the kissing gate, they turned north onto the path they could have chosen before. It followed the crest of the hill through meadowland with patches of overgrown gorse and small thickets, and meandered down the slope for more than a kilometre. Halfway down, the brush disappeared and meadowland spread into the bottom of a long valley where the main road, a railroad track and a river wound through it like wayward ribbons.

"That's the River Ugie, or rather the South Ugie Water," said Murdoch. "You can see the Abbey of Deer from here. That little bridge over the river leads to the road that goes past it." He pointed across the valley in the distance.

They could just make out the abbey ruins through some trees on the other side of the river.

"The May, 1308, battle stretched over this whole area," Murdoch continued. "It's a different bridge now, and this whole slope would have mostly been covered with grass and heath, though there might have been a few trees that they could have used for cover during the fighting."

Emily gazed across the landscape, imagining what the battlefield must have been like all those hundreds of years before. The scenery wavered in front of her eyes and she felt dizzy.

Suddenly dust and debris swirled around her and there was a mighty clash of heaving bodies everywhere she turned. Her ears rang with the cries of battle, the clanging of swords and shrieks of anguish. She cringed as horses charged past her, churning up clumps of raw earth. She smelled the sweat and fear of men fighting; saw the flashes of clubs and swords and axes as bodies fiercely hurled themselves at one another.

Distraught women and children dodged through a cluster of thatch-roofed huts huddled partway down the hill, racing for cover or heading towards the river. Their shouts and screams rose above the pandemonium of the men attacking each other, most of them on foot.

Without warning, a rider and horse headed straight

towards Emily, the wide blade of his claymore at the ready. She saw his face clearly and was sure he saw her. She screamed and pitched herself to the ground as he thundered by, the horse's hooves narrowly missing her head as she rolled out of the way.

"Emily, are you all right?" Dad bounded over to her.

She blinked, peering around. All was peaceful and quiet, except for the hammering of her heart.

"I'm fine," she said at last, but she could still taste the fear that had washed through her.

"What happened?" asked Dad, helping her to her feet. "One minute you're standing there and the next you bite the dust."

Emily blurted out the first thing that came to her mind. "I guess I tripped in a gopher hole."

Murdoch Lowry gave her a peculiar look. "There are no gophers in this part of the world."

"Well, maybe I tripped on a rock or something." She shook the debris off her clothes. "You know how clumsy I can be sometimes, right Dad?"

Dad said nothing.

Mr. Lowry gazed at her for a moment longer, then seemed about to launch into another story. But Emily wanted to know if the battle was somehow related to the woman from the stone circle.

"Are there any stories about the families of the men in the battle? Maybe one that involved the women or a particular woman?"

Murdoch Lowry thought for a moment. "As far as I ken, it was the men doing the fighting. There are stories and songs about the battles and such, but I've not heard anything special about the womenfolk."

She'd have to be more direct. "What about legends or ghost stories around the stone circle?"

"Aye, quinie, I see what you're getting at." Murdoch Lowry chuckled. "None that I've heard."

"What is this word, *quinie*, you called me?" asked Emily.

"It's a term of endearment, meaning girl or young woman. Some say 'lass,' but 'quinie' is also used by many people in this part of Scotland."

"Thanks." Emily smiled. "Were there any legends around the Abbey of Deer or the village of Old Deer?"

He shook his head. "Not my speciality. And if there was a hint of a legend, it would be common knowledge, passed down through the generations."

Emily tried again. "Were there other battles around here? Or stories about any special artifacts, like pottery or household items?" This was as much as she dared to say without directly asking about the mirror. And she could tell by the quizzical expression on Dad's face that he found her questions a little strange, too. She hoped she wouldn't have to explain about the mirror, at least not until she knew more about it.

"Nae again, quinie. Sorry. There were other battles

farther away from here and more recent, too, but nothing much was ever said about the womenfolk and children. Or everyday objects."

"That's too bad," said Emily, crinkling her forehead. "I wonder how the wives, mothers...and the sisters and daughters felt about the wars. How did they live while their men were away fighting?"

Dad and Mr. Lowry studied her as if they'd never thought about that aspect of history before.

"You know, Emily, you ask a very interesting question. I don't think history has ever captured much about how women endured battles and the loss of their families and homes," said Murdoch.

"Guess that's why they call it *his*-tory," said Dad with a smile.

"Groaner, Dad!"

"But he has a point," Murdoch said.

"This has been so interesting." Emily turned to Dad. "But maybe we should head back to Maud for lunch, before we go to the Abbey of Deer. It'll take us a while to walk back."

She hoped he'd take the hint to leave before Murdoch Lowry got talking again.

"Emily and I are on holidays, and doing a little family research. We want to see as much as possible in a short time," Dad explained.

"Well then, you'd best be off." Mr. Lowry nodded to them.

He gave them precise directions to the Abbey, indicating the spot on the map Dad drew from his pocket.

Emily edged away. "Thank you so much for your help."

"Thank you." Dad shook Murdoch's hand again.

"If you want to hear more about the *his*-tory of the area, just let me know," he said and started downhill.

"Thanks," Dad said and turned to Emily. "Guess we should have driven to speed things up."

Emily agreed, wishing she was back at the cottage checking out her mirror.

"I say." Mr. Lowry stopped a few steps away and turned back to them. "I don't mean to intrude, but if you'd care to, I could drop you back in Maud. My car's down on the road just around the bend, and I'm heading there."

Dad and Emily looked at one another and grinned.

"Sure," they said together.

Going downhill was much easier, with only a few rough bits along the trail, though it still took a good half hour. Emily hardly noticed the time, because Murdoch Lowry kept up a constant patter.

"Until the middle of the twentieth century, the lower part of the hillside was also the site of the largest horse fair in the north of Scotland. Traditionally held on the third Wednesday of July, Aikey Fair Day was regarded as the great summer holiday."

Emily broke into his story. "Why is everything called

Aikey Brae? I mean, I know a *brae* means a hill, but why Aikey?"

Murdoch smiled. "Ah, the legend is that a dubious character by the name of Aul' Aikey dropped his pack while crossing the River Ugie and he spread out his belongings from it to dry at the bottom of the hill. A good many people passed during the day and offered to buy what he had. Delighted with his unplanned success, he promised to show his purchasers something better worth looking at if they would meet him next year at the same time and place. He kept his word, and returned year after year. Others wanted to make money, too, so traffic gradually increased until it became the most popular market for all of the district of Buchan."

"So this whole hillside became known as Aikey Brae?" Emily asked.

Murdoch nodded. "Yes, but these days the area is also known as Parkhouse Hill, because of the farm nearby. Even the stones are called Parkhouse Circle on current ordnance maps."

"How long ago did the fair start, then?" asked Emily.

"There are some that say it was started as early as the Middle Ages by the monks from the Abbey of Deer. Others date it to 1661, but seeing as how the conflict in the 1300s was called the Battle of Aikey Brae, I'd guess the peddler probably showed up before then, maybe even around the same time as the monks." He paused. "Either way, the fair expanded to encompass fifty or sixty acres right to the river. The area was covered with crowds of people, cattle, horses and tents with various kinds of merchandise."

As Mr. Lowry described a typical fair in the late 1800s, Emily imagined fairgoers spread out around them and pipers from all over the countryside. Amongst them, she imagined her ancestors, who must have lived somewhere in the area. She saw children calling for the "coriander sweeties" Murdoch described, and folks dancing on the grass to the skirl of the bagpipes. She watched merchants barter webs of sacking, bed-ticking, gaudy coloured prints and huge bundles of wool and yarn. She saw refreshment tents with hundreds of people milling about.

She didn't imagine the scene too hard, though, in case she was pulled into the past again. But by the time they reached the bottom of the hill, she wondered why that hadn't happened. After all, this event probably involved her direct family members, and the mirror had passed through their hands. Maybe she was wrong about how the visions worked.

"Did I hear you say you were doing some family research?" asked Murdoch Lowry, when they reached the road. "Perhaps I might be able to help you."

Emily explained about the Elliotts and how they'd been from Scroghill, though she didn't yet know where it was.

"The where is easy," said Murdoch. "You can see

Scroghill from the Aikey Brae standing stones."

"You mean it's that close?" Emily said.

"Indeed."

Dad chuckled. "We thought it would be a lot harder to find than that!"

Murdoch's eyes twinkled. "As I said, that part's easy. The family name, on the other hand, is not common around here. There certainly haven't been any of them living at Scroghill for a long time."

"How do you know that?" Emily asked. "Are you a family historian or something?"

Murdoch beamed. "Nae, quinie. But I happen to know someone who lives in one of the old manor houses. The estate used to be owned by the Earl of Glaslyn. He used to own several properties, and he also operated a mill and brewery."

"Wow, estates were big back then," said Emily.

"Aye." Murdoch nodded. "Finding if your great-grandfather bided there may not be so easy." He stroked his beard. "I do know that Laird Elgivin, as he's known hereabouts, has kept many of the old records. Maybe he would have something of use to you. I will check."

"It would be wonderful to find out what the laird has," Emily said.

Dad agreed.

"Do you think he'll mind looking for us?"

"Nae, quinie. And I can do better. I can take you there, and you can look for yourself."

"You mean I'd get to see a real manor house? And meet a real laird?"

"Certainly." He paused. "We could go this afternoon if you like."

Emily turned to her dad with a lifted eyebrow and a little smile. He nodded.

"We'd love to, Mr. Lowry," said Emily. "That is, if we wouldn't be intruding on the laird. You must know him quite well to be able stop in at any time."

"Nae, it'll not be a problem. It's settled, then." He strutted ahead of them, his kilt swinging about his bandy legs.

They'd nearly reached the car – a plush Bentley, Emily noted – when Murdoch stopped again. Looking a little flustered, he said, "I know this may be a wee bit presumptuous, as you hardly know me, but would you care to have a spot of lunch with me before we examine the records?"

Emily gave her dad what she hoped was a pleading enough look to persuade him to agree to this, too. Before her parents split, she could read him really well, but now his face didn't show as much emotion and she wasn't sure how he would react.

"That's very kind of you," Dad answered. "But we wouldn't want to impose on you at such short notice. Your wife might not take kindly to strangers dropping on her doorstep unannounced."

Murdoch gave a hearty laugh. "Never been wed, and

I like it that way. Saves a lot of grief. But I do have someone who cooks for me, and she always prepares more than enough."

"All right then, we'd love to join you," Dad said.

They decided Mr. Lowry would drop them off at their cottage and they could pick up their rented car and follow him to his home. He had an errand he wanted to run in Maud first, while they freshened up. He'd be back in half an hour.

What an opportunity! First day out and she might learn something about her grandmother's origins. And she'd seen the woman from the mirror on Aikey Brae, among the ancient standing stones.

CHAPTER FOUR

When Murdoch Lowry sped off, Dad checked his e-mails and Emily rushed to her room. She didn't have much time, but she didn't want to wait any longer. As she reached for the carved box, she heard Dad's cell phone ring. He'd be busy for a while.

Lifting the lid, Emily sat on the bed with the box on her lap and gazed inside at the jewel-embedded frame of the mirror. What had she done the first time that let her see the vision of the woman? And how had the woman come to her at the standing stones *without* the mirror? Was Emily doing something to make it happen without knowing it?

Another thought struck her. Each time she saw the vision of the woman, she seemed to be drawn more and more into it. And on the hillside, she'd travelled back in time to the ancient battlefield. If these things were happening without the presence of the woman *and* without the mirror, she had to figure out how it all worked. What if she got stuck in the past and couldn't get back?

Emily drew out the mirror and turned the glass upwards. She was looking only at herself. She hadn't realized how tense she'd been, yet she was a little disappointed, too. She smiled. Her hair was a mess. She picked at a strand that was on the wrong side of her part.

And it happened again. The mirror warmed in her hand and the glass went cloudy. Colours shimmered and a moment later the dark-haired woman in the threadbare clothes appeared. Emily's hand shook and the image began to fade.

She steadied the glass and watched as the woman's image came through more strongly. Her face was haggard, her body contorted in sorrow. She stared straight at Emily, arms outstretched, beckoning.

Emily felt as if she was falling into the mirror. All of a sudden, they stood face to face. The woman spoke.

"Find her."

Although the woman was speaking some ancient language, the words popped clearly into Emily's head.

"I don't know what you mean," Emily whispered, partly aloud and partly in her thoughts. She didn't know who the woman was or where she'd come from.

Emily felt herself slipping further into the vision, until she was beside the stranger on the open hilltop, outside the standing stones. The woman swept her arm over the panorama of the surrounding valleys and pointed in the direction of the old battlefield.

"Find her. Quickly."

The woman pulled the tattered shawl around her shoulders. She hugged her arms across her chest, dropped her head and began to weep.

"Find who?" Emily asked clearly, in her mind.

Kiresz.

The strange name came to Emily like a murmur, although she knew the woman hadn't spoken aloud. Who was Kiresz?

"Emily." Dad called from downstairs.

Emily jumped and jerked the mirror. All of a sudden she was alone, no longer part of the scene, and the mirror image had vanished.

"Coming," she answered.

She placed the mirror back in the box, and put it on the night table. She'd have to find out more later, if she dared.

Emily grabbed her journal and stuffed it into her backpack. Now that she'd been to the stone circle, she knew exactly where the woman was standing, and when. And now she had a name to go on, although it was unusual. But how could she find out more about her?

As she left the room, she heard the woman's voice: *Find Kiresz.* She closed the door and ran down the stairs.

Mr. Lowry stood in the front doorway with a look

of dismay on his face, shifting his tam from hand to hand. Dad's face seemed flushed.

"I'm afraid I have an urgent meeting in Aberdeen this afternoon," Dad explained to Emily. "The leader of my team needs to go over the plans so he can line up everything in time for the dig next week. I'm sorry, but we won't be able to go with Mr. Lowry."

"But I don't want to go to the meeting with you, Dad. There won't be anything for me to do." A flood of disappointment washed over her.

"Please try to understand how important this is, Emily." His voice had a tinge of pleading, mixed with impatience.

Emily gave him a look of disbelief. He was going to a meeting about some dumb rock-hunting expedition *during their holiday*. She clamped her mouth shut and glared at him.

Murdoch Lowry, cleared his throat. "If I may make a suggestion… It's a pity you have to work, Mr. Bradford, er, David, but Emily is still welcome to lunch and tour with me. I assure you she will be perfectly safe. I have a cook, as I mentioned. Perhaps you could visit some other time."

Emily was almost too upset to try to coax Dad, but the chance of seeing a manor house and meeting a laird was too much to pass up.

"I'd like to go with Mr Lowry. I wouldn't be any trouble."

Dad stood undecided. "I'm not sure that's such a good idea."

"Perhaps it would ease your mind," Murdoch said, "if you brought her to my home yourself and had a look around before you headed off. You could collect her at, um..." he wavered as if he'd lost his train of thought, "Laird Elgivin's estate at the conclusion of your business."

Dad nodded, relieved. "Thank you, yes, that makes me feel better."

"Good. I'll give you directions and you two can follow at your leisure."

Dad drew a piece of paper out of his pocket and jotted down the route. Emily became calmer. They'd both get to do what they wanted, but it wouldn't be together, and she wasn't happy about the way it had come about. When would Dad ever put her first?

"This is where you'll find me on the road to Stuartfield," Murdoch said, drawing a little X on the map. "Right here is Scroghill, which you'll need to pass to get to my place." He marked the second spot.

"Thank you," said Dad. "We shouldn't have any trouble finding you."

"I will see you both later. Whenever you arrive is fine." Murdoch Lowry settled his tam back on his head, ready to depart.

"Wait, Mr. Lowry," Emily said. "Could you please tell me about the etiquette for meeting a laird."

Murdoch Lowry let out a belly laugh. "I'm sure the owner will be delighted to have you as his guest just as you are, quinie."

Emily grinned and waved as he left.

DAD GATHERED WHAT HE NEEDED for his meeting and they headed to the car.

"Emily, what's with you and carrying around your full backpack?" Dad asked, as she stowed it in the back seat. "You could leave the heavy things in the cottage."

Reluctantly, she told him about the antique hand mirror and how she'd found it in Gran's house. She left out the bit about the special things she could do with it. "I'd rather take it with me to Murdoch's, so I know it's safe. Besides, I might find something out about its history there."

Dad shrugged, and a short time later, they were off. They drove along the same route they'd walked. As they drew near to Murdoch Lowry's, they came across a small stone house with two chimneys built into the side of a hill. Only the front wall was fully visible and it didn't seem to have a name on it.

"Stop," cried Emily. "I want to take a picture."

Dad jerked to a halt, pulling over as far as he could get onto the narrow edge of the road. "Be quick, then. We may have to move if a car comes."

Emily hopped out of the car, and crossed the road.

With a roar, a vintage MG sports car painted lime green sped around the curve towards her. She leapt aside a second before the teenager at the wheel would have knocked her into a gorse bush. As he passed, he suddenly saw her and his eyes widened. He slammed on the brakes with a terrible squeal and shot out of the car.

She looked back into the brightest green eyes she'd ever seen. The boy couldn't stop looking at her, but she didn't think it was love at first sight, it was something else.

"I'm sorry," he said. "I didn't see you." He brushed back his dark thatch of hair and Emily saw a flicker of a silver earring in one lobe.

"Maybe because you were going too fast," Emily said.

"Don't I know you?" he asked. "I could swear –"

"That was the worst driving I've seen in years!" David had come across the road, and he was shaking with anger. "You could have killed my daughter!"

"Yes, it was. I'm so sorry, sir. I'm Angus Peters –"

"I don't care who you are, that was disgraceful!"

"Dad, I'm okay." But she was shaking now, too. Dad was right. Angus could have killed her.

"Yes, I suppose you are. Well, young man, I expect you to slow down and be more careful."

"Absolutely, sir. My conduct was inexcusable. I'll have to do much better." Angus edged towards his car.

"See that you do," David called after him.

Angus drove off so slowly that Emily had to stifle a laugh. She picked up her camera where she'd dropped it by the road and turned her attention back to the small stone house. It was her reason for stopping and she wasn't going to let Angus spoil that.

Something about the small house enchanted her; the way the hill wrapped around it snugly on three sides, the flowering bush at one corner and windows that looked over the valley. It seemed warm and inviting, reminding her of home at her Gran's stone house. She felt especially drawn to the beds of pink roses that reminded her of the wild roses on the prairies.

She thought about asking for permission to take pictures, but the house had a closed feeling. There was no vehicle around and the curtains were drawn, yet it looked like someone took care of it. She snapped pictures quickly from several angles and got back into the car, satisfied.

The next place they approached was a bigger spread with a faded sign posted on one of the buildings.

"Scroghill!" Emily unbuckled her seatbelt.

"Emily, we don't have time. We have to be at Murdoch's."

"He said we'd be fine whenever we got there."

"We'll have to be fast." Dad stopped in the entrance to the yard. "Let's see if there's anyone home. Maybe they'll let us have a quick look around."

A driveway led between a two-storey frame house to

the left, and three long, low stone buildings joined at the corners to form an extended U-shape on the right. A friendly black Labrador wandered out to greet them, followed by a stout dark-haired man.

Dad introduced himself and Emily to the owner, Ian McPhee, and explained why they were interested in his house.

Mr. McPhee turned to Emily. "So your ancestors lived here?"

"Yes, that's what's in their records." Emily turned to the white frame house on their left.

"Your folks wouldn't have lived in that house — it's less than one hundred years old."

He pointed at the stone buildings. "Could have been there. I believe they're at least two hundred years old."

"It looks like three barns stuck together," Emily suggested. Was this what a croft looked like?

"Indeed, it was joined this way for warmth in the winter at some point, but originally, if the one section was used for the house, it would have been separate. Come along, if you'd like a closer look."

"Thank you." Emily followed Mr. McPhee towards the longest section.

"This was a typical stone building with turf and thatch roof." The owner opened the door. "The livestock would have been housed in here."

He led them through the dark barn. The wooden stalls were gone, but Emily found it easy to imagine cows chewing their cud under the high windows, chickens scratching in the straw and maybe a pen of sheep at one end.

"This led into the storage area," said Mr. McPhee as they came to a door in the end of the barn section.

They stepped over a timber threshold into the middle section, a low-ceilinged room, open from one end to the other. The whitewashed stone walls brightened the room. Mr. McPhee explained that this section would have been used for implements, and to hold grain and other supplies.

As they stepped back outside, they examined the third section, accessible only by a doorway from the outside. It was divided into two parts.

"I think this might have been the house section," said Ian McPhee.

Things didn't feel right to Emily, somehow. She tried to picture what it must have been like when her ancestors lived there. In the first room there would have been box beds, maybe with curtains. The other room had the outline of a huge fireplace, where they would have cooked their food. A table with benches probably served as their dining table and workspace.

She imagined children bringing in splintered logs or dried dung and peat for the fires. She saw them sitting at the table, chopping vegetables or learning their letters while their mother and older sisters mended clothing by the light from the tiny window. She pictured bunches of herbs strung to dry from the rafters, and a huge black pot of mutton stew hanging from an iron rod over the fire. Although her envisioned scenes seemed accurate to her, the feeling that her family had lived there was missing. Yet, if her great-uncle Geordie said they came from Scroghill, this had to be the right place.

"Do you mind if I take photographs?" she asked, deciding she'd record their time at the place until she could figure out why it felt all wrong.

"Feel free to take as many as you want."

He stepped out of her way as she began snapping sequential shots of the whole three-part structure. Whoever had built it was a masterful stonemason, proven by how well the building had endured into her own time. When she got to the barn section, she noticed a small doorway on the end and peered inside.

"That room was called the *chaw*-mer." Mr. McPhee said. "Spelled the same as your word chamber. It housed an unmarried man who worked on the farm in exchange for his meals and a small wage."

"There's not even a window," Emily said, entering the cramped room.

"He'd only sleep in here, though he might have brewed a little tea. He'd take his meals with the family."

"How would he manage in the winter?" The small fireplace built into the wall would hardly have kept him warm with the high ceiling open to the rafters.

"Well, it wouldn't be that comfortable with the

cauld weather, but he'd have somewhere to bide, all the same."

Emily shuddered. She couldn't imagine living here at any time of the year.

"How could he even read a book in here?"

"It would have been by candlelight. But he wouldn't be able to do that very often," said the owner. "Candles were hard to come by, and so were books."

Dad explained. "They used tallow candles – made from the fat of sheep and cattle – and there wouldn't have been much to spare for candles."

Mr. McPhee nodded. "They apparently didn't smell very good, either."

Emily shivered. "How could they live like that?"

"They lived as best they could, and it was difficult. They seldom had even enough to eat, especially when they had to give large portions of their crops to their lairds if they had no cash to pay their rental fees."

"Rental fees to lairds?" Emily asked.

"Scroghill Farm was part of a large estate owned by the Laird Elgivin."

"Yes, I know that, but I thought they worked the farm for the laird, got to live here and made a wage."

Mr. McPhee shook his head. "Nae, your great-grandfather might have bided here as the grieve – the manager of the farm – but he had to earn his way. Rent was always owed."

Emily fell silent.

Even Dad seemed surprised. "I didn't realize that a feudal type of landowning system existed into the late 1800s."

"Oh yes," said Mr. McPhee, "And even into these modern times, although we'll soon have a law to end it. Nowadays, many landowners are selling off parcels of their properties, which is how we bought this place."

"Did you find any old papers or belongings from the previous residents?" Emily asked.

"Nae, we haven't come across anything in these old buildings. They were stripped bare when we moved in."

"Did you ever hear any stories about the Elliotts?"

Ian McPhee shook his head. "Nae. I don't know any history of the place or people."

"No stories about special belongings that may have been handed down in families?" Dad suggested.

"Or legends from around here," Emily added.

Dad looked at her curiously again.

"Or maybe, uh, ghost stories or something like that," she added lamely. Dad was getting suspicious of her questions. If she didn't want him to know about her visions, she'd have to be more careful in what she sad.

"I'm sure there's many a ghaist left haunting the old battlefields and buildings hereabouts. The local history societies might have something."

"It was a thought, anyway," said Dad. "Em, I think it's time we got on our way. Thank you for your time, Mr. McPhee."

Emily thanked him, too, and they headed back down the driveway. Dad had called her Em, the way Mom did. Maybe he did remember the old times.

"Wait a minute now," Mr. McPhee called after them. "I do remember one mention of a wraith...a story about a young maid being sighted on this very stretch of road by people in buggies or riding horseback. She seemed to float beside them for a bit, as if she was looking for someone."

"Do you know what she looked like?" Emily asked.

"Some say she had long dark hair, and a long dress maybe, and it only happened at night and in the spring. This was years ago."

Was this the woman from the stone circle?

Emily looked across the valley to the hills in the northwest. Although she couldn't make out the standing stones, she could see the trees on the hilltop and knew the ancient circle was standing guard there.

Little by little she was learning more about her family and about the woman in the mirror. Were they connected somehow? Maybe Laird Elgivin would have some answers.

CHAPTER FIVE

Are you sure we took the right turnoff?" Emily
glanced at the hand-drawn map again.

"That's what Murdoch told me." Dad continued
down a sweeping road beneath a canopy of trees.

"There doesn't seem to be any other road to take,"
Emily said.

Without warning the road widened and they
were in an open meadow area. Straight ahead was a
formidable castle in the middle of well-tended
grounds stretching several hundred metres in every
direction.

Dad braked to a stop. "This can't be right."

"Turn around quick, before someone sees us," said
Emily.

"I'll have to go around the driveway," said Dad.
There was nowhere else to go. Just as he pulled even

with the tall, double oak front doors, one of them opened.

"Oh-oh, they've seen us," said Emily.

"We might as well ask for directions." Dad stopped the car.

Murdoch Lowry stepped outside, still in full Scottish clan regalia.

Emily and David sat speechless.

"I thought he gave me directions to *his* home and that you were going to the laird's place *after* lunch," said Dad.

"He must have marked the map wrong or changed his mind," Emily said.

Murdoch waved his arm to indicate that they could park anywhere. He greeted them warmly and led the way into a grand foyer.

Emily felt almost as if she should curtsey, but decided it might be more appropriate to save that for when she met Laird Elgivin. Instead, she peered at the broad columns that towered above her, at the expansive marble floors, and the huge urns of full-grown trees reaching through to the second floor.

"I hope we're not late," Dad said. "We made an unplanned stop at Scroghill."

"Ah, so you've seen the farm. That's good indeed. Did you discover any information of interest?"

"Sort of," Emily said, still not as excited about Scroghill as she'd thought she would be.

Dad glanced at his watch. "I'm afraid I don't have

enough time to stay for the tour."

"That's quite all right, David. You can look around when you come back for Emily."

"Mr. Lowry," Emily interrupted, "I'm confused. I thought we were having lunch at your place first, then going to Laird Elgivin's to look at old records. Will we come back here later for Dad to meet us?"

"We'll be here..." Mr. Lowry seemed to stumble over his words.

They all jumped when someone cleared their throat to the right of them.

The elderly woman's lined face held no smile. She wore a plain rose-coloured shift with a stiff collar and a starched white apron. Her salt-and-pepper hair was coiled at the nape of her neck. She seemed a little distant, but her brown eyes showed a certain cordiality.

"Excuse me, Laird Elgivin, would you be wanting luncheon served in the dining room or the library?"

Emily scrutinized her host. "*You're* Laird Elgivin? *You're* the Earl of Glaslyn?" she squeaked. Part of her wanted to tell him off for tricking them, and part of her still wondered if she ought to curtsey.

"Aye, that I am."

"But why didn't you say so?" Emily crossed her arms over her chest.

"I wanted to have a normal conversation with the two of you for a while. I didn't want you think about me having a title, like you're doing right now."

"I see your point," Emily said.

He turned to the housekeeper. "We'll have lunch in the library, please, Mairead, and there will only be two of us."

"Very good, Laird Elgivin." The housekeeper turned back the way she'd come.

"Now that the ferret's out of the bag, so to speak, shall we continue?"

Dad chuckled. "Very good, *Laird Elgivin!*"

"We'll have none of that. Please call me Murdoch, both of you, or I shall not be able to – what's that North American term – hang about with you." There was a twinkle in his eyes.

"Hang *out,*" Emily said.

"Fine, uh, Murdoch," said Dad. "I'll be off." He gave Emily a brief hug. In a moment he was out the door.

"Now, Emily, shall we store your backpack in the hall closet?"

"I'll keep it with me," she said. "I'll probably need it later." Besides, she didn't want the mirror out of her sight.

"As you wish," Murdoch said with a smile. "We'll finish the house tour first, and after that we'll have lunch, then look at the records."

With a sweeping gesture of welcome, he showed her the way, his kilt swaying around his short, hairy legs, making her think of a stubby wrestler, or a warrior from ancient times, not a privileged laird of the manor.

They crossed the great entrance hall and entered a

long, elegant passage with polished stone floors. Emily's sneakers made squeaking sounds like pips from frightened baby squirrels. "This is a true fortressed manor house built in the seventeenth century," Murdoch explained. "Not one of those upstart Victorian shooting lodges built with turrets to look like one."

She nodded. She'd never seen either kind before, but apparently the difference was important to him.

"It was built for defence, not as a home, but over the centuries, it has been remodelled for comfort."

They entered a magnificent ballroom with sparkling chandeliers high above them. Golden sconces gave subdued lighting over plush-covered armchairs. China ornaments and large vases with huge flower arrangements covered small tables. At one end of the room, a suit of armour stood guard by the massive fireplace. A hand-carved mahogany balcony ran across the other end.

"For the orchestra," Murdoch said, looking upwards. "Though we haven't had use for one for many years." His voice echoed off the high ceiling.

"This is a huge place for only you and a housekeeper," said Emily.

"Indeed, we have most of the rooms closed off," said Murdoch. "There used to be upstairs and downstairs maids, two cooks, a scullery maid, a butler and footmen and a coachman. Now Mairead does for me and I hire local people for any occasional cleaning work that needs to be done."

"Sounds sensible," Emily answered.

"And less costly, too," Murdoch said.

They toured around the perimeter of the ballroom. Large paintings hung along the walls. Murdoch pointed out portraits of his ancestors.

Emily quit listening when she caught sight of a painting of a woman and child, in an alcove near the fireplace. She felt drawn to it with such intensity that she hardly noticed Murdoch's voice droning on behind her. He stopped finally, to watch her progress to the far end of the room.

The dark-haired young woman in the painting wore a long, full-skirted gown and sat on a high-backed chair. The young girl standing at her knee had the same dark looks and style of dress as her mother. They looked so real that Emily felt as if she could reach out and touch them, and they might come to life and hold a conversation with her. Their eyes held her gaze even when she moved to the side.

"Superb isn't it? Everyone admires this painting," said Murdoch Lowry, coming up beside her.

The woman's eyes seemed familiar. "Is this a relative?" Emily asked.

"Yes. An ancestor."

"On your mother's side," Emily said with certainty.

"Yes." Murdoch looked startled. "But how could you know?"

"I just had a feeling." Emily gazed up at the painting

and suddenly understood its power over her.

"Her name was..." Murdoch began.

"Kiresz." Emily whispered it to herself. The dark oval eyes were those of the woman in the mirror.

"What did you say?" Lowry asked, his sea-blue eyes rounding in surprise.

Emily repeated the name, louder this time. This lady looked more refined and more recent than the woman in the mirror, but the resemblance was uncanny. Although Emily didn't know the mirror woman's name, she was looking for someone named Kiresz, who must be related. Maybe the mother and child were her descendants.

Murdoch gathered his wits, giving himself a shake, almost like a dog ridding itself of water after a dip in a lake.

"Well Emily, I have to say you've taken my breath away. How on earth you could know that is beyond me."

Emily didn't know how she knew either, she just did. But the knowing scared her, too. She stumbled about for words to explain.

"A lucky guess, is all," she finally said, shrugging.

"She's fey," Mairead's voice came from behind them. "She has the second sight."

Emily turned to find the old housekeeper, wheeling a trolley holding a silver teapot, china teacups, tiny sandwiches and dainties soundlessly across the room.

As she drew closer, she gave Emily a probing look, sending chills through her. Maybe the woman didn't like her for some reason.

"Shall we stop for lunch?" Murdoch took Emily's arm in his.

"Indeed," Emily answered, playing the part of the lady of the house. The housekeeper followed behind.

Murdoch escorted Emily into a long, wood-panelled room and guided her to a chair by the fireplace, where a small fire burned briskly. He took a seat opposite her with a low, claw-footed table between them.

The housekeeper passed Emily a three-tiered plate filled with a choice of sandwiches and a variety of dainties. As Emily helped herself, her eyes locked on Mairead's.

At first the dark grey eyes looked stern, probing into hers, but then a ripple of softness appeared before she broke contact and moved away. Emily felt a strange connection and a curiosity.

As Murdoch poured the tea, Mairead quietly left the room.

Emily felt like she was in the middle of some movie set. And she was still surprised about seeing the painting that resembled the woman in the mirror. Murdoch hadn't forgotten either.

"So quinie, tell me when you first realized you had the gift of the second sight."

Emily shrugged. "I didn't really know I had it until

maybe recently," she said, truthfully. She hadn't thought about her past experiences of travelling back in time in that way.

"Have you noticed any other unusual phenomena in your life?"

Emily almost giggled. She wasn't about to tell him about the mirror or what had happened at the ancient battlefield. He might not mind that she had the "second sight," but she didn't want him thinking she was completely weird.

"My mother always said I had great imagination. Maybe some things are more real to me than to most people."

He watched her intently. "Kiresz is a name that was passed down in our family for several generations."

"It's not a name I ever heard before I came to Scotland," said Emily.

"Indeed, it's not a common name here, either. Outside of my family, I know of no others. The Kiresz in the painting lived over a hundred and fifty years ago, but there were others after her."

"So what year was the painting done?" Emily asked.

"I believe the date was 1819." He reached for the teapot and topped up their cups.

"She reminds me of someone I've seen before. Is she famous for anything?" Emily asked casually.

"Not that I'm aware of," said Murdoch. "She was said to be a kind, good lady, who loved flowers. She designed the gardens you now see on the estate."

Emily glanced towards the French doors.

Murdoch rose and led her outside onto a fieldstone patio that fanned into a wide set of shallow stairs. A stone walkway led to brilliantly coloured flower gardens intersected by grassy paths with secluded seating areas under large, draping trees.

The flowerbeds weren't nearly as well pruned and orderly as she'd expected to see on a laird's estate. One had heather, tansy and yarrow tangled with wild grasses. Another brimmed with yellow primroses and white-flowering brambles.

There was also a herb garden where she recognized St. John's Wort and other medicinal plants. The most surprising section was a smattering of pink roses along the walkways, the same as she'd seen at the stone house with the two chimneys. Murdoch noticed her interest in the delicate pink flowers.

"Eglantine roses," he said. "Favourites of Kiresz."

Emily bent to smell them. "They're like our wild roses on the prairies."

They came to another low flowerbed jumbled with harebells, fairy flax, violets and field pansies. The unruly wildflowers reminded her of home and her walks with Grandmother Renfrew in the pastures. And was that a fairy-tale gazebo she could just glimpse near the edge of a pond? The white structure with pergolas and latticework railings was almost hidden by some kind of climbing ivy.

"Are these gardens similar to when she first created them?" asked Emily.

"Yes, and we've maintained them as well as we could, although some species have likely changed over the centuries."

"They are lovely," said Emily. "I'm sure I would have liked her."

Murdoch beamed. "I'm sure my great-great-great-grandmother would have liked you as well."

"Do you know anything else about her?" Emily asked. "Maybe some stories handed down through the family?"

"Not that I recall," said Murdoch, leading Emily back inside the manor house. "She was often referred to as the "gypsy" of the family because she liked to dash about the countryside visiting people, and to travel abroad at least once a year. She was constantly moving things in the house, too."

Emily decided she'd have to be more direct if she wanted specific answers. "What is her family history?" she asked, as they seated themselves in the library again.

"I'm afraid I don't know much about that. I never thought to ask when my grandparents and parents were alive, and now it's too late."

Murdoch passed the tiered plate again and she chose a fruit tart.

"Brambleberry tarts. One of my favourites." He took

one for himself. "You really must try the shortbread, too," he added. "Mairead makes some of the finest I've tasted. And you'll think you've died and gone to heaven when you taste her sticky toffee pudding."

"You're lucky to have her in that case," said Emily.

She glanced across to the opposite end of the room at a rosewood desk with papers and books lying on it.

"You're lucky to know so much about your family, too," she prompted, hoping this would bring the conversation back to her research.

He nodded, taking the hint. "Yes, and that's why you are here. As soon as we've finished our lunch, we'll take a look at the papers."

"Great." She wiped some crumbs from her mouth. "So the name Kiresz, is it a Scottish one?"

"That's difficult to answer. Scottish names come from many sources. There are five different dialects of Scots, as well as Gaelic, Norse, Cumbric, Pictish, Doric, and English, of course – plus names from other cultures that invaded the country, including European and Scandinavian ones. So I'm not entirely sure of its origins."

"'Tis a Gypsy name." The voice from behind startled them both.

"Ah, Mairead. I didn't hear you come in."

"That's a positive thing, then," she answered primly.

Emily wondered if the older woman was being sarcastic, but Mairead kept a straight face.

She glided over to the tea trolley and lifted the lid of the teapot. "Would you be wanting some more hot water for your tea?"

Murdoch shook his head. "No, that will be all, Mairead. Thank you."

"The lunch was delicious, especially the tarts and shortbread," Emily said, smiling at the prim woman in the starched white apron.

"Glad you enjoyed them, quinie." Mairead's face lit up momentarily, and then she gathered their lunch things, placed them on the trolley and left the room as quietly as she had come.

"Crepe soles," Murdoch murmured. "That's how she sneaks up on me."

Emily laughed. "Has she been with you for long?"

"Yes," said Murdoch.

"Why is she certain Kiresz is a Gypsy name?"

With some reluctance, he said, "It's not the name itself, it's that she has some romantic notion that she herself has Gypsy blood and likes to think others have, too."

"And does she?"

"Perhaps a tiny drop. As far as I know her parents are Scottish, but I indulge her and let her think I believe it." Murdoch rose. "Shall we move to the writing desk? I have some things laid out for your examination."

CHAPTER SIX

Emily followed him and sat down in a chair he'd placed beside his. She saw a neat stack of papers, books and a journal set to one side of the desk.

"Please tell me again about your family that lived at Scroghill."

Emily repeated what she knew. When she finished, Murdoch placed an old journal in front of her.

"Wow, this is ancient!" Her hand hesitated over the kidskin cover.

Murdoch nodded encouragingly. "Please open it."

Inside, the writing was tiny, like a squirrel's scrabbling in the dirt and just as difficult to decipher. Murdoch grinned and handed her a magnifying glass.

"I think you'll find this helps."

The glass made the words bigger, but they were written in some old dialect, and she still couldn't make them out.

"This doesn't look like a personal diary," Emily said.

"No, it's a journal with daily entries about the workings of the estate. More like what you might call a ledger."

"Your family was one of the wealthiest around here, wasn't it? And my family would have been lucky to work for them?" Emily couldn't keep a sharp edge out of her voice. She didn't want to feel less important because her family had been poor.

"Er, well yes." He paused, a little embarrassed. "Now that we have that issue out of the way, shall we continue?"

He bent over the journal again. Emily watched him run his finger down the pages, mumbling the names of each tenant as he went. She caught glimpses of names, lists of crops planted and harvested, what they'd been worth.

Murdoch read up to 1875. "The Elliotts must have come a little later, if they're here at all."

"They left for Canada in 1899, so it would have been before that." Emily looked at the lists.

"Here!" Murdoch jabbed a spot on the page. "George Elliott, Scroghill, 1876. Eighteen years old."

"That's my great-grandfather." Emily said, excited.

"He's listed as a chamber."

Emily thought about the small dark room at the end of the barn at Scroghill. Her great-grandfather must have lived there. She shuddered.

"Here's another entry." Murdoch's "rrrrs" were coming thicker as his excitement increased. "He must have married, because in 1878 he's listed as a crofter and only married men were allowed to have a croft." He turned the page.

"Ah yes, here it is...his wife's name was Margaret Elsbeth. She sold eggs to the estate."

"Yes, Margaret Elsbeth Sangster. She went mostly by Elsbeth in Canada, as there were several other Margarets in their district," said Emily. "Does it say exactly where they lived?"

"Looks like he had a croft with six acres."

"So he didn't live with his family in any of the Scroghill Farm buildings we saw this afternoon?"

Murdoch shook his head. "As a chamber he would have, but after he was married he obviously took over a croft – one of the smaller places on the farm. There were six of them, by the looks of it."

"Does it say which one?" Emily knew which house she wanted it to be.

Murdoch scanned several more pages. "Nae. There isn't much more information about your family. By 1899, when they left, they had eight children." He flipped to the ledger section and passed it to Emily. "The writing is easier to read now."

She followed the entries year by year. George Elliott had been heavily in debt, and by the last couple of years, unable to pay any of his rent. No wonder they'd left for

Canada still owing money to the laird. And the descendant of that laird sat right beside her.

He patted her arm. "It's bleak, I know. But look at all the others in the same position." He pointed to other families' records. No one had been able to pay much of anything for several years.

"But what happened to all the families?"

"Some left, like your ancestors, and some, I suppose, were turned out."

"Where would they go?" She imagined families with their belongings in sacks on their backs, starving, begging on the roads, sleeping in ditches.

"They'd try to find work elsewhere, I suppose. Some emigrated to North America, or went to the poorhouse with nothing more than the clothes on their backs."

"How horrible."

"At one point the government helped some people sail to North America," Murdoch said. "Others had help from the churches or special organizations."

Maybe that's how her grandmother's family had managed, but that kind of information wasn't recorded.

"But if your tenants didn't have anything to give you — well, the lairds at the time — what did the families who owned the estates do to survive? Or did they have enough money and food so it didn't matter?" She wanted to understand things from the landowners' viewpoint.

His expression was sad. "Even though an estate

might be large and worth a great deal of money, most owners didn't have much in the way of actual cash, and still don't. According to these records, we had to sell things eventually, including some property, so we could buy food and pay our taxes. There is no doubt those were lean years, and we rationed what we had, but we obviously survived." He seemed embarrassed by the affluence surrounding him.

"Our neighbours on the Aden estate were almost decimated. There were several deaths in the family, and in this country, every time someone dies, a certain percentage of the value of their estate is paid for death taxes."

Emily leaned back into her chair, thoughts whirling. What a strange system of landowning they had in Scotland. She was glad that her ancestors had come to Canada.

Somewhere in the distance a grandfather clock chimed four. She couldn't believe so much time had passed since she'd arrived.

"Now, is there anything else I could show you while you're here?" Murdoch asked.

Emily hesitated. She wanted a chance to speak to the housekeeper. "I'd like to see where Mairead works."

Murdoch looked surprised. "How unusual. Are you sure?"

"Yes, please," Emily said, lifting her backpack onto her shoulder.

"I suppose if that's what you'd like to do..." Murdoch

wasn't smiling any more. "Follow me, then."

"Thank you," Emily said, wondering why Murdoch seemed reluctant to let her visit Mairead. Was he keeping something back from her? She considered abandoning the plan, but curiosity won out.

He led her to a narrow stone passage to the kitchen.

Before he opened the kitchen door, Murdoch said, "Mairead is bound to fill your head with Gypsy lore, but it's all rubbish."

"I'll keep that in mind," she said, "but I love to hear stories, even if they're not true." Was he worried Mairead would tell her something important?

When Murdoch opened the kitchen door and stood back, Emily was greeted by the scent of cinnamon and ginger, and inviting warmth, from the oven and from the fireplace at one end of the low-ceilinged room. It reminded her of Grandmother Renfrew's home. In one corner sat a rocking chair with a braided rug underneath to keep feet warm on the stone floor. Near it was a captain's chair with a needlework cushion. Copper-bottomed pots hung from an iron rack and herbs grew on the wide windowsills above the deep kitchen sink.

Mairead pushed the kettle onto the wood-burning stove.

"Welcome," she said. "Please sit."

"I'll leave Emily with you, Mairead," said Murdoch. "I have a couple of phone calls to make, but afterwards I shall return for her."

"Certainly, sir. We'll have some tea when the kettle boils."

"Remember what I said about Gypsy lore," Murdoch warned Emily.

"I'll keep an open mind," Emily smiled, though she was worried that she'd upset her host.

Murdoch disappeared. Emily took the captain's chair by the fireplace, tucking her backpack beside her feet. Settling into the chair, Emily waited for Mairead to speak first.

CHAPTER SEVEN

You've been having some strange visions lately, I'll be bound."

A shiver ran up the back of Emily's neck.

"You're here to learn what you can about your family." Mairead looked straight ahead, as if listening to something unseen.

Emily nodded.

"You wonder if the visions you've seen are connected to your family." Mairead closed her eyes.

Emily held her breath, waiting for more.

"They are, but not in the way you think."

This conversation was more like what a Gypsy fortune teller might say than a chat, but Emily didn't want to stop the flow.

"The family you are here to seek is not the one you will come to know." Mairead opened her eyes again.

"What do you mean?" Emily asked. The little hairs

on her arms tingled.

"You'll find out soon enough, especially if you continue to use the mirror." Emily nearly jumped up. "How do you know about the mirror?"

Mairead smiled. "It's part of the legend. My mother told it to me when I was but a child at her knee."

"How come no one else seems to know about it?"

"'Tis a private tale passed down through families."

"Do you know how old the mirror is?"

Mairead got up and fiddled with making tea while Emily sat on the edge of her seat, hardly able to contain her excitement.

The elderly woman bustled about the kitchen, checked the doneness of a spice cake in the oven and prepared a plate with raisin scones, butter and jam and the pot of tea. She seated herself in the rocking chair.

"For you to understand the legend of the mirror, I first have to tell you some long forgotten history." She gazed across the kitchen as if looking far back into time.

"Hundreds of years ago, around the year 800 AD, a sect of people from the warrior classes of northern India were driven from their homes. They made their way through Persia and into Egypt, where they wandered for a number of centuries, until their origins were obscured from common knowledge."

Emily shifted in her chair, wondering what lost people from India could possibly have to do with her family in Scotland. Mairead looked at her sharply, and

Emily paid closer attention.

"As displaced people without a home or country to call their own, they remained nomadic, and eventually, in the Middle Ages, they left Egypt and continued their trek northwards through the Roman Empire and thus to many European countries."

She turned and looked at Emily again.

"Because they'd been in Egypt for so long, Europeans referred to them as..." she paused for effect, "Little Egyptians or..."

Abruptly Emily understood. "Gypsies!"

This must be one of the stories Murdoch had warned her about. Emily felt a quiver of excitement. Though she felt Mairead was playing at being mysterious, she was sure there was a seriousness about her, too.

"They refer to themselves as Roma or Romani, though this has nothing to do with the country of Romania. There are also different kinds of travellers, and not all who are referred to as 'gypsies' are Roma."

Emily nodded.

"But when many people hear the term 'gypsy,'" Mairead went on, "they think of something negative, because a small number of travelling people became thieves and cheats, or because their lifestyle forced them to scrounge to make a living."

Emily reached for another scone and munched on it while Mairead continued her story.

"The Romani 'gypsies' became known for crafting

small household goods, for tinkering – repairing pots and pans – and other trades easily done within their travelling life."

"What other trades?" Emily interrupted.

"Things most other people didn't want to do, such as chair-bottoming, basket-making, rat-catching, wire-working, grinding, making earthenware and mending bellows."

"Wow, they did lots!"

"Aye, they were good with their hands. They also became renowned for their fiddling, singing and dancing. Sometimes they made their living entertaining people, and they were skilled with horses."

Emily had a sudden flash of a colourful, wooden-trimmed Gypsy wagon travelling down a country lane. She could almost hear the fiddle music and singing within, the clanging of tin pots and pans and the jangling of horses' harnesses.

"But they became most famous for their fortune-telling," Mairead went on, "because they had great powers of second sight."

Mesmerized now, Emily pictured what she thought of as a Gypsy woman, with a scarf tied around her forehead, big circle earrings, and dangling bracelets, seated in a tent behind a table upon which sat a large crystal ball.

She realized Mairead had stopped talking.

"Please go on," she said. Why was Mairead telling her any of this?

"There is little more to tell, except that some were brilliant craftsmen, having learned about metallurgy and the elemental compounds from ancient times. By the time they reached Europe, their work had become refined, though not well-known by today's standards."

"When did the Romani come to Scotland?" Emily asked, sure that Mairead was hoping she would.

"Some families made their way to this area of Scotland more than seven hundred years ago." Mairead fell silent again.

"Is that all there is to the story?" Emily asked.

"Nae, patience, quinie." Mairead poured more tea for them both and once more picked up her story.

"Among those families, there was a man who did such metalwork. He also brought with him some fine stones, passed down in his family for many generations. They'd been payment for work done for some great ruler. He made a beautiful object to honour his lovely young wife and to signify his intense love for her. This, too, was handed down to subsequent generations.

"I will let you think about this for a time." Mairead sipped her tea.

"Wait," Emily said. "You can't stop now."

Mairead smiled kindly, though she obviously wasn't going to say anything more for the moment.

"At least tell me what the gift was that he made for his wife."

"Do you really not know?" Mairead spoke with a

slight smile on her lips.

Realization struck Emily. "The mirror?"

Mairead gave her a look of satisfaction.

"The same one I have?"

"According to legend, it is the very one."

"How do you know?"

"Do you not feel it is so in your bones?"

A shiver ran from the bottom of Emily's spine to the nape of her neck. "But how did it come to me?"

"Ah, that is the biggest question of all. One your destiny will lead you to understand."

"Do you know the answer?"

Mairead shook her head. "Not all of it."

"Does this relate to you somehow? Or to Kiresz from the painting?"

"That is of no consequence to what you need to know at the moment." Mairead took their cups and plates to the counter.

"Is there more you can tell me?"

"Perhaps. But not now."

"Why not?"

"Laird Elgivin is coming to fetch you."

Emily listened, but heard no sounds in the passageway. However, she didn't doubt Mairead's powers of perception.

"I'm only here for a few more days," she pressed Mairead.

"You must have trust. The answers you seek will be

revealed through the mirror, and it will all happen in good time," the housekeeper said.

Murdoch entered the kitchen at that moment.

"My apologies for taking longer than I expected, Emily," he said, concern showing on his face. "I hope I didn't leave you too long."

Emily stirred. "No, our conversation was fascinating."

Mairead moved to tidy the kitchen, with a secretive smile.

"Learn anything to help you with your family search?" He watched her face as if looking for signs of some kind of revelation.

"Mostly history of how people came to Scotland," Emily said, not wanting to upset him by talking about Gypsies. "I'd like to hear more sometime," she added.

"That can be arranged," Murdoch said. "Emily, your father called. He'll be here in a few minutes."

"Okay." Emily picked up her backpack. "Oh, I almost forgot. Do either of you know Angus Peters?"

Murdoch frowned and his lips went tight.

With a sniff of disapproval, Mairead said, "He's not one that's willing to work for gain and he has great ambitions."

"Why do you ask?" Murdoch said.

Emily explained how Angus had nearly run her down.

"Reckless scoundrel," Murdoch said under his breath.

Mairead shook her head. "Sad, really."

"Too true," said Murdoch. "But let's not let talk of

him spoil your visit."

"It hasn't," Emily assured them. "This has been the most amazing time ever."

Murdoch smiled and headed to the door.

Emily turned to Mairead. "Thank you for a lovely visit."

Mairead held Emily's hands in her own and gazed into her eyes. "You're a bonny wee lass."

Emily hugged Mairead. "I hope to see you again soon."

"You can count on it. Now go. *Dewlessa*."

Emily gave her a questioning look.

"It's from the Romani language – a Gypsy word for goodbye. It means 'with God.'"

"Dewlessa," Emily said in return.

She followed Murdoch back down the passageway. As they returned to the ballroom, a rapping came at the front door. Dad stood there, looking drained, a smile pasted on his face.

"Hi Dad! How'd it go?" Emily asked.

"Fine. We're all set for the dig." He turned to Murdoch. "But I'm afraid I don't feel up to a tour of your beautiful manor right now."

"Never mind," said Murdoch. "I'm never far from home and you're welcome any time."

"Thank you so much for helping my daughter, Laird Elgivin, uh, Mr. Lowry, uh, I mean Murdoch."

"We've had a grand time. l look forward to the next

time. And Emily must come back for another visit with my housekeeper. They seem to have hit it off rather well."

Emily gave Murdoch a playful curtsey. "See you again soon, Laird Elgivin."

She heard his laughter as she took her father's hand and walked him to the car.

Going back to the cottage suited Emily fine. Her thoughts swirled with all the information she'd gathered, and she wanted to make some notes.

Meeting Mairead was one of the strangest things Emily had done in her life. And seeing the resemblance between the woman from the mirror and the Kiresz in the painting was the most amazing. It certainly looked like the two women were related, but how could she find the connections between them?

Emily leaned her head against the backrest. The day had been long and she was exhausted. She closed her eyes.

Without warning, Dad slammed on the brakes and swerved. The car skidded to a stop. Emily screamed as a woman's face appeared at the passenger-side window, then disappeared.

CHAPTER EIGHT

W hat happened?" Adrenalin pumped through Emily's veins so hard her ears throbbed.

Dad's face and knuckles had gone white.

"I thought I saw someone pop up from the side of the road." He clenched the steering wheel. "I thought I was going to hit her."

They peered around, but the landscape was the same, late afternoon sun casting a warm glow on the hills around them.

"There's no one there now," Emily observed, calming herself.

Dad got out and walked up the road. Emily checked in the other direction, but there was nothing out of the ordinary.

"I must be more tired than I thought," said Dad with a wobbly laugh. "I'm seeing things that aren't there."

"What did she look like?" Emily asked, although

she'd seen the woman, too.

"Dark hair past her shoulders, a shawl over her head. I didn't have time to take it in." He ran his fingers through his hair. "Daydreaming, I guess, or probably just seeing things."

"Maybe she was the ghost Mr. McPhee talked about."

Though she'd only seen the face for an instant, Emily was sure it had been the mirror woman. Dad's description seemed to clinch it. But why had she appeared now? And why on the road?

"Nice try, Em," Dad said, obviously still a non-believer in ghosts and other things unexplainable to his scientific mind, though his face still held the look of shock.

Emily contemplated whether to admit seeing her, too. She didn't want to tell him about the strange powers of the mirror or the vision she'd seen at the stone circle. Besides, he'd never believe her!

Instead, she went over in her mind what questions she was going to ask the next time she met the woman from the mirror. She was wide awake now, and determined to find out more.

Dad drove more alertly, too, and it wasn't long before they were back at the cottage. Soft hues of fading daylight slanted over Maud, outlining the trees and rooftops.

Before they could alight, a tall, stocky woman with

bright red curls down to her shoulders strode towards the car, reminding Emily of a female Viking warrior. All she lacked was the metal helmet.

When they'd first arrived, their landlady had left them the key under the doormat, because she was going to be away until late, so they hadn't met her yet, though it looked like they were about to.

Emily scrambled out and joined Dad at the trunk of the car where he was unloading the groceries he'd bought in Aberdeen.

The Viking strode over with a broad smile.

"Peggy Kerns." She took a firm grip of Dad's hand, towering over him. "You'll be David Bradford. And this will be Emily." "Kerns" came out like "cairins" and she rolled the "rrrrs" in Bradford.

"How do you do?" Emily's hand was engulfed in a vicelike grip.

"My apologies for not being about when you arrived, but I see ye found the place and are getting settled in. I'd just like to give ye a wee tour to explain a few things."

Peggy led them through the second floor bedrooms, the bathroom, the kitchen and the living room that opened into a sunroom, all in a matter of minutes. She showed them where the extra bedding and towels were kept and how to open and adjust the windows and shutters. They didn't like to tell her they'd already discovered all these things.

Peggy Kerns also showed them the light switches,

the hot water switch for when they wanted to take a "wee" bath, the breaker box and the cupboard with the spare bulbs, and she explained how the washing machine in the kitchen worked and where the clothes-line was in the garden. She told them the best food store was only a block away. And that they could get good meals at either the tea room or the pub.

"But I can't go in the pub," Emily said.

"Aye, ye may at that," said the woman, with a sudden smile. "Even wee bairns are welcome."

"We'll give it a try in that case," said Dad.

"You look all flattened. Shall ye want some wa'er on the hob for a spot a tay noow then?"

They shook their heads, not quite sure what she meant.

She patted David's hand. "If you need anything while you bide here, coome roon' ta the hoose across the way. Ta."

And she was gone, leaving them in sudden silence.

Dad and Emily burst out laughing.

"Did ye ken wha' she said?" asked Dad.

Emily collapsed on the sunroom window seat. "I think my brain's still trying to catch up."

"I think if we need anything we're to go over to her house," Dad said.

"And apparently I can go in the pub," Emily added. "In the meantime, shall we ha' some wa'er on for a spot o' tay?"

Dad laughed. "How about we wander down the street and find a spot of supper instead?"

All tiredness forgotten, Emily sprang to her feet, realizing she was hungry again.

"Fancy a little haggis?" Dad asked. "Scotland's national dish, ye ken."

"Not on your life." She'd checked the Internet. Haggis was made of sheep's heart, lungs and liver cooked in a sheep's stomach with oatmeal and herbs, and she didn't want any part of it.

"I'll take my oatmeal in the morning, cooked as porridge."

They sauntered down the sidewalk, admiring the tiny closed shops on the narrow street. They all seemed to run together in one long attached building: a butcher's, a bakery, a hairdresser, a computer store and finally the grocery store and post office.

Emily felt a rush of excitement. She was going to an old-fashioned Scottish pub. She'd heard stories of days gone by when famous travellers and horse-drawn coaches pulled up so passengers could have a meal or rest the night. Would the Station House pub still have some resemblance to those days?

They entered the high-ceilinged pub, crowded with people at trestle tables in booths or on stools at the long oak bar.

"Hiya." The youthful barmaid smiled as they approached the bar. "What can I get for ye?" She pointed to a chalkboard propped in one corner, which announced the day's specials: *cod and chips and peas, meat pie with peas and chips, or sausage roll, peas and chips.*

"I guess I'll have the chips and peas..." Emily grinned at her dad.

"And?" His eyes twinkled.

"With the sausage roll." She wished for a plain hamburger instead. "Oh, and an orange juice."

She looked for a place to sit, but all the tables were full.

"You're welcome to sit at the bar, until a table comes free," the barmaid said.

"Thanks, er...I'm sorry I don't know your name," said Dad.

"Stella." She smiled and reached over the bar to shake his hand as he introduced them.

"You'll be the folks staying at the Nicholls Cottage run by Peggy Kerns."

"That's right." Emily looked at her in surprise.

Stella laughed. "News passes quickly in this wee village. You'll find that almost everyone is connected in some way through family ties, except for newcomers, and even some of those find they are related." She winked at Emily. "Besides, it's the only place available to stay right now, except for the hotel here, and it's full."

Stella went off to place their food order, and returned in a moment with their drinks. "So what brings you to this area?" She definitely wasn't shy either.

While Dad explained their trip, Emily sipped on her orange juice and listened to the conversations buzzing around her. A middle-aged couple planned their shopping trip to Peterhead for the next day. Two teenage girls with spiked hair and piercings all over their bodies discussed what they were going to wear at some rock concert at Inverness.

Emily heard the words "family tree" and "Elliotts" and turned her attention back to the conversation beside her.

"I've never heard of anyone by the name of Elliott living around here lately," said Stella. "But you could check the headstones over at the parish cemetery."

"Where is it?" Emily asked.

"When you step out the door, look straight ahead and you'll see the spire. Keep it in sight 'til you get there. The kirk is no longer in use, but the cemetery is still kept up."

"Most of the older folks would have been planted there," said a voice in her ear.

She whirled around to face Angus Peters.

"You'll find all our families there," said Angus.

"Find them where?" asked Murdoch, crossing the bar to join them.

"Hello, Laird Elgivin," Angus said. There was an edge to his voice Emily couldn't understand.

"Hello, Murdoch," Emily said. "We're talking about the cemetery."

Murdoch greeted the others and sat on the stool on the other side of her. He rolled his eyes as Angus continued to watch her.

Emily shifted on her stool. She wasn't used to an older guy taking such an interest. Angus must be at least five years too old for her. She caught Dad's face reflected in the mirror. It was tight with anger.

Murdoch seemed to sense the discomfort among everyone. "This is Emily's father, David Bradford," he said pointedly.

"We've met," said Dad, relaxing somewhat.

"Hello again, sir," Angus said, slipping onto a stool. He looked again at Emily.

With an effort, she pulled her gaze away and turned back to their conversation. Out of the corner of her eye, she saw Angus looking at her reflection with a puzzled expression.

Stella said, "The prominent families in the area were the McClintochs and Robertsons."

"If any Elliotts married into one or the other of those families, you'll be able to tell soon enough," said Murdoch.

"Did I hear mention of the McClintochs and Elliotts in one breath?"

A tall elderly man with spindly legs like a flamingo approached the bar with a sour look on his face. His greying hair fringed a pinkish bald spot on the top of his head.

"Do you know of them?" Emily asked.

"Aye, that I do. But those two families never married one another. They'd as soon spit in each other's eye."

"Why do you say that?" Angus swung around and confronted the older man.

"Old resentments never die. My gran knows a thing or two about that." He eyed Emily and her dad with a slight tilt to his head, reminding Emily of a quizzical bird.

"Harry Starke." He darted his name out and waited to hear theirs.

As Dad made introductions, Harry Starke wedged an empty stool between them and Angus.

"So there were lots of Elliotts living around here at one time?" Emily asked.

"Yes. Stella, my usual, please," he ordered.

The barmaid nodded and lifted an eye towards Angus for his order. He pointed to a bottle on the shelf. Murdoch also made his request known.

"So how does your gran know so much about the Elliotts?" Emily asked, as Stella poured the drinks.

"Was one of them, wasn't she."

"An Elliott?" asked Emily, as Stella set their food before them.

Starke glared at her through dark, beady eyes. "Aye, Gran was an Elliott, but married a Robertson. Proud of the family name, she was." He thumped the bar again. "The Robertsons and the Elliotts go a long way back.

They stuck together against the McClintochs during the Jacobite rebellions and have ever since."

"Didn't those uprisings take place in the 1700s?" Dad asked.

"Started in 1688; ended in 1746." Harry sucked on his ale.

"Well, then, but that's a long time ago," said Dad.

"Can't get nothing past you, can we?" Harry Starke smirked.

Emily couldn't keep from giggling. Angus chuckled too. Even Murdoch hid a smile.

"Dad means that it seems a long time for families to hold grudges."

"That's as may be, but it's the way it always was, and always will be!" Harry's black eyes simmered and his hawklike nose flared as if he was about to peck them.

"Now, Mr. Starke, don't get your feathers ruffled," said Angus.

Murdoch added, "I'm sure they don't mean anything by it."

"Not at all," said Dad, putting a hand on Emily's shoulder in a protective way. "We're curious, is all. We didn't mean to offend."

"That's all right, then." Harry Starke looked straight ahead at the mirror behind the bar, his sharp eyes wary, like a bird in a tree watching the progress of a cat on the ground. He only stopped when Stella brought his food.

"Do you think we might be related?" she asked.

"Not very closely, I'm sure," he said, as if he hoped they weren't related at all.

"But I thought the families stuck together."

"They usually did," Angus butted into the conversation.

Harry Starke gave Angus a withering look, and turned to Emily. "They must have been a different branch, or I would have heard about yours."

He shifted ever so slightly away from her, pecking at several peas with his fork.

Darn, she'd offended him again. She was beginning to wonder if she wanted to be connected to him, either.

She gave a quick glance into the mirror at Angus, deep in thought. A moment later, a look came over his face, as if he'd figured something out and things were falling into place. He said nothing. She wished she knew what he was thinking.

"I don't know anything about *your* Elliotts," Harry Starke started again. "Obviously, they are not part of the main Elliott family."

Emily felt deflated. "Who would know something about my family's branch?" she asked, not willing to give up.

"Wouldn't your gran know, Harry?" Stella asked.

"She's still alive?" Emily blurted out. He looked too old to have a living grandmother.

Harry Starke swivelled in her direction. "Certainly. We are long-livers in my family."

Emily suppressed a giggle, imagining a long, skinny piece of liver. She heard Angus snigger. Mr. Starke glared at him.

Angus backed away in mock fear. "Okay, I'll be going, then. I know when I'm not wanted." He winked at Emily.

Emily felt her face flush and she looked down at her plate. Angus was good-looking, and he knew it, too.

"I hope to see you again, Mistress Emily Bradford." Angus bobbed his head goodbye, his green eyes sparkling.

Emily wasn't sure if she wanted to see *him* again. His charm was definitely overdone, though she found it hard to tear her eyes away from him.

"One moment, Angus," Stella said. "There's the small matter of the bill."

"Put it on my tab, please, Stella," he said.

"It's getting a little long."

"I'll pay next time I'm in," he said with a wide smile.

He swaggered out the door with a quick glance at the young teenage girls, who whispered across the table to one another, staring after him with interest.

Emily thought she heard Murdoch say something like "young hooligan" under his breath, but she couldn't be sure.

She turned back to Harry Starke. "Could you ask your gran about the Elliotts for me?" she asked, as politely as she could manage.

He looked at her sharply. "She has her good days and her bad days. Her memory isn't always reliable. After all, she is ninety-eight."

"If you could try, I'd really appreciate it." Emily gave him a big smile.

He darted a look at himself in the mirror behind the bar, patted his hair and turned back to her.

"All right, I'll visit her and ask your questions. I'll be in contact if I have anything for you."

"Thank you!" Emily took his hand and shook it hard. He shrank back, she suspected from embarrassment. "We're staying at..."

"Nicholls Cottage." Starke stood down from the stool.

"What was your great-grandfather Elliott's first name, if you don't mind my asking?"

"Alexander."

"And who was his father?" She couldn't keep the excitement out of her voice.

"I don't know." Starke withdrew a few coins from his pocket and set them on the counter to pay for his half-eaten supper.

"Do you think your grandmother will know?"

"Could be, but I make no promises." He nodded to them and strutted out like a flamingo darting into the water.

"I suppose there's hope there," said Emily, eyeing Dad's doubtful expression.

At least it was another direction for her to explore. And she wanted to find out all she could about her ancestors and the origins of the mirror before her time in Scotland ran out.

CHAPTER NINE

The aroma of blueberry pancakes and bacon wafted up from the kitchen early the next morning. Emily jumped out of bed and joined Dad.

She finished cooking the bacon and placed it on the dining-room table next to the butter and syrup. Dad shoved his papers into a pile in a corner and set the plate of pancakes in the centre of the table.

Emily twirled a bite of pancake in the syrup and popped it into her mouth. "Mmm, this might be your best batch ever."

"It does taste pretty good, I have to admit," said Dad. "Probably because we're hungry after a good night's sleep."

"Maybe, but I'm sure glad you made your famous pancakes."

"This bacon is great too, Em. Not too crisp, yet well done."

A pang of homesickness hit her for the way things used to be, all of them working together in the kitchen on weekends: Dad doing most of the cooking while she and Mom took care of the extras. Then she realized that hadn't happened for a long time even before her parents had split, but it was something she would remember when she thought of her family.

Maybe there was something she could do to bring her parents back together again.

After breakfast, Emily washed the dishes and Dad dried.

"Can I ask you something?" Emily said.

"Shoot." Dad reached for a plate from the draining tray.

Emily hesitated. "Do you think you and Mom will ever get back together?"

A mixture of emotions crossed over David's face. "I know you'd really like that, Em, but, no, that's not possible. There's too much water under the bridge between us."

He placed the plate in the cupboard with care.

"What do you mean, water under the bridge?" Did he have to use his silly sayings every time he talked to her?

He grabbed a handful of cutlery. "Your mom and I have been through a lot and we're just too different now to be able to stay together."

A sudden jab of pain cut across her chest. "Does it have anything to do with me?"

Dad put his hand on her shoulder and turned her to face him. "Look at me, Emily." He looked directly into her eyes. "What is going on between your mother and I has absolutely *nothing* to do with you... None of this is your fault."

Emily bit her lip to keep back the tears.

"Please don't ever think that. We both want the best for you."

"So there's nothing I can do to stop this from happening?" She held back a sob with a wet, soapy fist.

"No," Dad sad quietly. He dried the knives and forks and put them back in the drawer.

He put his arm around her shoulder as she turned back to the sink. Taking a long deep breath, she washed a glass, and handed it to him.

He dried it slowly. "I'm sorry this is happening to you, Em."

Several salty teardrops slipped into the dishwater. She scrubbed at her eyes with wet hands, making her whole face wet. The ache in her chest increased, but she took several gulps to force it back down. She wished her dad would hug her and everything would be okay. She just wanted to go home and live like a family again.

The silence in the room was broken only by the swishing of Emily's cloth and the clatter in the sink. She couldn't even glance at her dad.

Suddenly he said, "Looks like company coming."

She looked out to see Angus Peters sauntering across

the street towards their cottage. She hastily dried her face with another tea towel as Dad answered the door.

"Good morning, Mr. Bradford, Emily."

"Please come in," invited Dad.

Emily held back, knowing her face was all blotchy and red.

"Thank you, but no, I'm on my way to a look at a job," he said, standing just inside the doorway and boldly glancing past them into the kitchen, the dining area and up the staircase. "You've made the place very comfortable for yourselves."

"Yes, we're settled right in," said Dad. "Sure you can't stay for a few minutes?"

"No, thank you. I've just stopped to tell you that I've been over to the cemetery at St. Mary's and I've found some Elliotts." He played absent-mindedly with the doorknob. "Not sure if they're your ancestors, but at least there are a few names and dates that might help you trace them. Most of the headstones are in the southeast corner, though they're not all together."

"Thanks, Angus," said Emily, looking at him directly for the first time. His eyes were a piercing jade this morning. She looked rapidly away.

"That was nice of you," Dad said.

"Maybe it will help make up for my bad driving." Angus glanced into the cottage once more. "Good luck with your research." His eyes searched Emily's, but she avoided looking directly at him. "Well, I'll leave you to it, then." He gave them a wave and headed off.

"Would you like to go there now?" Dad asked, though she saw him glance towards his laptop.

"I could go and you could check your e-mails."

"But I don't want you on your own in a strange place."

"Dad, look around you. The pub is right down the street, and I have to pass Maud Primary School and several businesses. It's bright daylight. I'll walk through the cemetery, take a few photos and be back before you know it."

"What if someone approaches you?"

"I'll say hello." She grinned. "Really, Dad, nothing will happen to me. I'll go straight there and back, promise."

Dad looked towards the kirk. "I guess it would be okay. But if you come across any trouble, scream loudly or run and get me."

Emily rolled her eyes. "It'd be faster if I just headed to the pub or waved down that police officer." She pointed to a uniformed policewoman getting into a marked car.

Dad kissed the top of her head and ruffled her hair. "Off you go. See you in a while."

"See you later, Dad."

Had Dad just sighed? Emily looked both ways and crossed the street without a backward glance. This would be a snap. After all, what could possibly happen at a cemetery in the middle of the day?

She headed down a curved cobblestone street towards the church spire, past a small pond with swans floating on it, and soon reached a waist-high fieldstone fence, enclosing St. Mary's Kirk and the grassy, L-shaped graveyard.

Inside the front gate, Emily passed through a newer section of polished marble gravestones dating from the 1940s. The next section was older, but still too recent to contain Elliott family graves.

As she moved on, many of the tombstones seemed to be toppling or had already fallen. Some were made from soft stone that had crumbled easily. On the more weathered ones, the names were totally missing. Moss grew on them, and in places, patches of black mildew obscured letters and numbers.

A sudden breeze set a swing in the playground swaying and the chain clanked against the metal seat. Emily had a sense that someone was watching her, but when she glanced around, there was no one. She drew her hooded sweatshirt closer.

She made her way to the southeast corner, where Angus Peters had told her to look, and began to search for the Elliott name. She was amazed to find dates going as far back as the mid-1700s. There were so many, and time and nature had taken them over, pushing, sliding and pulling at them, so that the ground was uneven and they sat at odd angles.

But there were none older than that, and she gave up looking for the ancient Kiresz name amongst them. The Kiresz from Murdoch's painting seemed a better bet, but the Lowry ancestors didn't seem to be here either. Where were they buried? She pushed the question aside. She'd be lucky enough to find some of her own family.

Turning to the next row, she tripped on a vinelike weed, its tendrils climbing up a marker.

And then she saw it.

Andrew Elliott was carved in wide letters on a tall tombstone, jutting above the others. She brushed away some of the debris and found the dates *1829–1892*. Below this was an inscription, *Beloved husband of Janet Forbes Elliott*. She had found her great-great-grandfather, the father of George Elliott who had lived at Scroghill. Emily raised her camera, taking close-ups and long shots from various angles.

She noticed several small headstones with lambs carved on top. One read: *Jane Elliott, 5 May 1768 – 18 June 1769, aged one, In the Arms of the Angels*. It stood beside a headstone for *Ada Elliott*, who had died at age three, only a few days after Jane. Next to it was one for *Thomas Fraser Elliott*, who died two weeks later. How sad to lose so many children at one time.

Perhaps they all succumbed to some sickness that had gone through the family. Something similar had happened to the Elliotts when they first settled on the

Canadian prairies. In 1899 both her great-great-grand-mother and her great-aunt Emma had died from a flu epidemic.

Emily found two adult headstones nearby, probably the children's parents. She read: *Beloved father and husband, Robert Gibson Elliott, 1733–1810.* Beside him lay his wife *Elspet Robertson Elliott.* Her birth year was either 1731 or 1737 and the death date was obliterated altogether.

Here was also proof that the Elliotts had been linked to the Robertsons, just as Harry Starke had said.

After that, everywhere she looked there were Elliott markers. And she found more Robertsons and Harry Starke's relatives, and other names he'd mentioned, like McClintoch. And there was one person who had Elliott as the middle name. She snapped a quick shot of the Robert Elliott Peters headstone. Maybe this was some relative to Angus Peters. Was she distantly related to Angus as well?

A dark cloud passed overhead, blocking out the light. Somehow it gave the place a sinister feeling. She bent to take one last photograph.

A hand touched her shoulder. She screamed and whirled around, clutching her camera with both hands raised in front of her, ready to swing.

Harry Starke's narrow hawklike face loomed in front of her, his eyes covered in shadow from his dark hat.

CHAPTER TEN

Didnae mean to frighten you. Just wondered how you were getting on." He tilted his head and studied her, like a crow on a fencepost. "Saw you from across the pond."

She glanced over his shoulder to the other side of the water where a flock of goosanders – diving ducks – huddled in a sheltered spot. Someone *had* been watching her. Surprisingly, she felt relieved knowing she hadn't imagined it.

"It might have been better if you called out," she said, a touch of annoyance in her voice.

He shrugged in agreement, then shook himself like a bird ruffling its feathers. "Did you find some of your Elliotts?"

She nodded. "Plenty, but I need to know how they're connected."

He hesitated for a moment, as if trying to make up

his mind. "My gran confirmed that your relatives are connected to ours."

"I was sure they had to be."

"Yes, well, but your branch of the family splintered off from ours. She doesn't know much about them, though she knows they eventually went to the wilds of Canada."

"Yes, that was my great-grandfather, his mother and his family," Emily reminded him. "But why did they separate in the first place?"

"More just that there wasn't enough land to support two families, and a question of rights of the oldest, my gran said."

"I don't understand."

"My great-grandfather Alexander Elliott gave his brother George the push from the tenant farm. And rightly so," he added, shifting from foot to foot.

"What do you mean?" asked Emily.

"That's the way things were in those days — still are to some extent. The oldest inherits and the younger siblings must fend for themselves. It was time for George to make his own way."

"But that's horrible!" Emily said. "How could someone do that to their own brother?"

"They had to survive. Alexander had eleven offspring to feed and he had to make provision for them."

"But George was only fourteen," Emily said, amazed.

Harry shrugged. "He found work for another land-lord, didn't he? Got married, had a family…"

"The crops were so poor several years in a row that they couldn't pay their rent. They *had* to go to Canada," Emily said.

Harry Starke shrugged as if it made no difference to him.

"So George's family never tried to help him out at all?" Emily asked.

"They wouldn't have been able to."

"But wouldn't they have wanted to keep in touch?"

"I doubt it. Especially, when their mum, my great-great-grandmother, turned their back on them and decided to emigrate with the younger son."

"She was my great-great-grandmother, too!" Emily spluttered. "And I'm sure she wouldn't have turned her back on anyone. More likely she went with the one who appreciated her the most."

Starke open his mouth to say something, then closed it again.

"I knew we had a connection," Emily said more quietly. She did some quick calculations, trying to figure out what relationship Harry Starke would be to her.

"Yes," Starke admitted with some reluctance. "But it's quite a ways back."

Emily sighed and changed topics. "Do you know why one of the Elliott ancestors would have the *middle* name of Robertson or why someone else would have Elliott?"

"Middle names? Why, er, yes. Children were often given a middle name to identify their ancestral ties."

Emily looked at him blankly.

"I am referring to the old custom of naming the first two boys and the first two girls in a family after the four grandparents. The elder son was named after the grandfather on the paternal side – meaning the father's side – and the next after the grandfather on the maternal – or mother's side. The elder daughter was named after the paternal grandmother and the younger after the maternal grandmother."

"That might help me trace the family," said Emily.

"Perhaps." He turned on his heels to leave.

"I bet your grandmother would know how it all fits together," Emily called.

"I doubt it." He answered over his shoulder. "She doesn't want to be bothered with such questions." He stopped.

"Maybe I could visit her, seeing as how we're related."

"Nae, that wouldnae be possible." Starke seemed upset. "She doesnae see anyone but me. She isn't interested in meeting you or knowing a thing about you."

"She actually said that?" Emily asked in disbelief.

He darted away on lanky gull-like legs, not stopping or turning back again.

Emily glanced at her watch. Time to get back before Dad came looking for her. She took one last look over the cemetery and headed for the cottage. She kept glancing over her shoulder to make sure no one was behind her. She didn't like to admit it, but Harry Starke had frightened her.

When she opened the door a few minutes later, everything was silent. She found Dad snoozing in a reclining chair in the sunroom, snoring softly, his work papers on his chest. She crept up to her room. She needed time to digest the information she'd uncovered. More importantly, she wanted to do some more exploration with the mirror.

Sitting on her bed, Emily pulled the looking glass out of the carved box. How had it come into the Elliott family and afterwards into her hands? According to Mairead, the way she could find out more was through the mirror.

Emily's fingers trembled a little as she caressed the stones and decorative metalwork, sensing the loving workmanship the maker had put into it. Using a tissue, she cleaned the gemstones.

She'd have to ask her dad for sure, but she thought the blue ones were either lapis lazuli or sapphires, and the red might be garnet or ruby, while the green ones could even be emeralds. If she was right, the mirror was extremely valuable, and if that was the case, why hadn't the mirror been sold to help the people who had owned it over the centuries? Surely they could have used the money it would bring?

By the time she was done polishing, the gemstones sparkled and the mirror felt warm in her hands. She took a deep breath, turned the mirror over and held the glass up to her face. Only her own image showed at first. She waited, confident in the questions she wanted to ask. The glass blurred and a swirling haze appeared, and then the glass cleared.

The woman appeared, her face filling the frame.

"What's your name?" Emily asked before the image could speak to her. *Larianna.*

Emily was ready with the next question. "Are your people Gypsies?"

Yes, Romani.

Did your husband make the mirror? Now Emily formed the questions in her mind only.

Yes.

Why have you come to me?

You must find Kiresz.

Is she a relative? Emily recalled the resemblance of this woman to the Kiresz in the painting.

The woman wrapped her arms in front of her chest as if cradling an infant, then brought her hands together over her heart.

Was she looking for her baby daughter?

The woman nodded.

"You want me to find her?" Emily whispered, leaning closer to the mirror.

The woman nodded again, her eyes filling with tears.

"What happened to her?"

The woman raised her shoulders in total anguish and helplessness. She wrung her hands, pleading.

Find her. Quickly.

The suffering in her voice was clear in Emily's mind.

"Where do I look? When did you lose her? What happened to you and your husband?" Emily fired more questions at her.

The surface of the mirror clouded and swirled. The glass cleared and Emily saw men in ancient battle garb, claymores and axes clanking against shields, bodies lying on the ground covered in blood. She heard the pounding of hooves, men shouting and running, and in the distance the beating of a single drum. At the top of a steep hill, a rider with a lance and raised standard surveyed the scene below.

Go there.

The scene disappeared and the glass cleared.

"What battle is it?" Emily asked. "Is it the Battle of Aikey Brae?"

Emily clasped the mirror in both hands, willing the woman to reappear. The glass stayed clear.

Emily closed her eyes and pictured the battle scene again. The standard the lone rider carried had a small flag, bearing a coat of arms with a stylized blue lion. Whose emblem was it? She had to find out if this was the Battle of Aikey Brae. The colours had been distinct. Maybe someone would recognize it.

And what about Larianna's child? She'd been so close to getting the answers she needed. Now what was she going to do?

"Ready for the Abbey of Deer?" Dad called.

Emily jumped. "I'll be right down."

As she loaded up her backpack, she felt a strong urge to take the mirror with her, thinking she might have a chance to visit Mairead somewhere along the way and could show it to her.

CHAPTER ELEVEN

Emily and Dad pulled up to the abbey ruins. A high stone wall encircled the ancient site, though parts of it had fallen into disrepair. They stepped over to the entrance, a grand gate with a stone portico and Doric columns.

A shiny lime-green MG whizzed in with Angus Peters at the wheel. He stopped with a squeal of brakes.

Rolling down his window, he said, "Good morning. I see you are out touring bright and early."

"Yes, we thought we'd get an early start," said Dad.

"Making a full day of it?" he asked.

"That's the plan," said Emily, hoping Dad would stick with it.

"I'd guess you're off to work?" Dad asked.

"Nae, I'm my own boss. I do odd jobs and work the hours I want to work. Taking care of a little other business today. So what are you hoping to find?"

"Just being tourists," Dad said.

Angus's eyes turned darker. "I suppose you'll be checking out more places to do with your family research?"

"We're not sure where we'll end up," Dad said. "It's up to Emily."

Angus nodded, a serious expression clouding his face.

Emily stood shyly to one side. She couldn't think of another word to say.

"Well, I'd best be off. I'm sure I'll see you again along the way." He flicked a strand of dark hair off his face and flashed a smile at Emily.

Emily still wasn't sure if she wanted to see him again.

Angus stepped on the gas, gave them a wave and disappeared from sight, headed towards Maud.

Dad shook his head and laughed. "He certainly likes to be charming."

"He thinks he is anyway," said Emily, catching the glint of amusement in her Dad's expression.

Once inside the gate, they saw that all that was left of the church and its other buildings were a few walls and the outlines of the foundations in stones. From the plaque that held a diagram of the layout, Emily read the list of buildings aloud while she and Dad matched them to the site – "lay brother's quarters, chapel, presbytery, latrines, chapter house and dortors."

"Dortors are the monks dormitories," explained Dad, anticipating her question.

"Thanks."

A partial wall with a doorway into the abbey kitchen still existed, as did the walls of the dining hall, below which the cellars, now filled in, had been. The Abbot's House and the infirmary were a little better preserved, though none of them had any floors or vaulted ceilings left. In places, part of the wall enclosing the churchyard had crumbled and fallen. Beyond it, fields and pastures spread over the hills as far as Emily could see.

Emily walked across the grounds and through the outlines of the buildings, looking for interesting angles for photographs. Dad walked in the other direction, trying to take shots from as high as he could to show the layout.

As Emily came to the wall at the edge of the ruins, a high chain-link fence stopped her. She sat on a low section of the foundation and looked out at the fields. The quiet peacefulness was broken only by the slight gurgling of a nearby brook and the whirring wings of a ptarmigan in the yew trees behind her. Overhead a flock of starlings soared.

Something dark moving on the distant hillside caught her attention. It drew closer, becoming a male figure in a dark hooded robe, clutching a bundle of sticks. He headed along the hilltop until he reached two small white crosses. He stood before them with his head bowed, then walked down the hill towards her. She lost sight of him behind a stand of trees.

She watched for a couple of minutes, but he never emerged. Perhaps he'd turned in another direction. There must be an active abbey in the neighbourhood. She'd have to ask where it was. Maybe the monk would know some old stories about the area.

Emily headed to the southern cloisters. When she rounded the corner of the Abbot's House, she froze.

A monk with his head bowed, holding a bundle, was only a metre away. Was he the man on the hill? If so, how had he gotten here so fast?

She opened her mouth to speak, but the figure turned abruptly and moved through an arched doorway into the ruined abbey kitchen. She followed him in, and instantly the room was as it had been in centuries past — with finished walls, high vaulted ceilings and long rows of trestle tables. The mouth-watering aroma of roasting fowls came from heavily laden spits in a fireplace at the other end of the room, where the monk dropped his bundle. Sticks clattered to the ground in a heap. He bent and stacked them by the hearth.

By the time Emily reached him, he'd gone out another door.

"Wait." Emily reached out to touch his robe. But the cloth slipped away from her fingers.

A split second later, the place was empty and everything lay in ruins, open to the sky.

Why had she slipped into the past? What could the abbey have to do with Larianna? Part of her wanted to investigate more, but most of her didn't. Wavering in and out of another time spooked her.

"Dad," she called. She couldn't see him anywhere.

"Dad!" she called again.

"I'm here, Em." Dad waved from across the grounds, where he'd been exploring a piece of carved stonework.

She hurried over to him. "Did you see anyone else walking around here?"

"Not a soul."

"Not even a monk?"

A puzzled look came over his face. "Uh, no. Are you okay?"

"Yeah, fine... I just wondered, that's all." She glanced over her shoulder. "Do you know if there are any other abbeys around here?"

"I doubt it, but we can certainly find out."

"And I know just the person to ask." Murdoch was bound to know. Maybe they'd see him at the pub later. She'd had enough of the Abbey of Deer for one day, and it was almost time for lunch.

"Let's go back to the cottage," Dad said. "Maybe if you sorted through all the information you already have, you could narrow down the things you need to look for."

Emily agreed. She did have a lot of notes she wanted to write and the entries from the cemetery to consider.

As they passed through the abbey gate, Emily shivered, glad to be leaving the ancient monastery. Every day weird things were happening to her and they all came from different sources. Were they all connected somehow?

"SOMEONE'S BROKEN IN!"

Emily stepped through the cottage door first. Although the place looked reasonably tidy, things were different, pushed about.

Dad moved past her and examined the table with his papers even more scattered than usual and his laptop sitting akimbo. The kitchen was mostly undisturbed, but they found the side door slightly open.

"This is where they got in," Dad said, examining the lock.

"Should we leave it alone until the police have seen it?"

"Definitely," Dad agreed. "Let's do a quick check upstairs before we call."

Emily moaned as she stood in the doorway of her room. Closet doors gaped and her clothes, pulled from their hangers, lay in a jumble on the floor. Her luggage was open and the contents spilled in messy piles. The bedding had been stripped and the mattress was askew, as if someone had searched under it.

"Can you tell if anything is missing?"

"Hard to tell from here." Emily gaped at the chaos.

Dad eased her out of the room. They looked in his room next, with much the same results.

Back in the dining room, Emily asked, "But what could they have wanted?"

"Whatever it was, I don't think they got it. It had to be something in particular, because they left my laptop and other valuables, including my cash." He held up a pouch with extra money still intact.

"The mirror!" Emily exclaimed.

Although she'd told Dad about the mirror, he didn't know how old it was and that it had valuable stones in the frame. He also didn't know about the strange things that happened when she used it. Either someone else must know, or the person wanted it because it was an antique. She was sure the mirror was what the intruder had come for. What other reason could there have been?

"How could anyone have known about it?" asked Dad thoughtfully. "I never mentioned it to anyone. Did you?"

Emily shook her head vigorously. "But someone guessed! Someone knows the history of the family and figured it out! That's the only explanation." She described it and explained its age.

"It's probably very valuable. Too bad we never had a chance to find out."

Emily grinned. She patted her backpack, which was still on her back. "Good thing I took it with me!"

Dad smiled with relief. "Maybe I should take a closer look at it."

Emily pulled the mirror out of her backpack and handed it to Dad.

"Amazing." He was awestruck, as he turned it over to look at the ivy designs in the metalwork. "We should probably get it appraised and take better care of it."

"Maybe an appraiser could give us a little history on it, too."

"Right. First things first...let's go find our landlady and get her help in calling the police."

Peggy Kerns was mortified that such a thing had happened on her property and to her guests.

"I can't imagine who would do such a thing," she said, thinking hard. "Someone took quite a chance for me not to see them."

"So you didn't see anyone suspicious?" Dad asked.

"No, and I have a good vantage point, too, with my kitchen window facing your way."

The whole process of having the police over to investigate, taking statements and doing a quick search for evidence took over an hour. The police confirmed that whoever broke in knew what they were looking for, and they weren't just kids tossing the place. The lock, not of the highest quality, had been easily jimmied.

Their landlady insisted she would do a thorough cleaning and tidy everything while they were out for lunch – on her.

"It's the least I can do," she said, vowing, "I'll have

the door fixed and a new lock installed by end of the day."

They left her to it and headed to the pub, hoping to find Murdoch Lowry. Emily wore her backpack with the mirror stowed safely inside.

CHAPTER TWELVE

Hiya," Stella called from the far end of the bar, with her usual big smile.

Angus Peters watched them approach in the mirror, turning only when Emily and her dad sat down at the counter a couple of stools away from him. He seemed unusually quiet.

Or was it Emily's mood that made her think that way? She sat with her chin in her hands and elbows on the counter, not saying a word.

Stella saw their expressions. "Oh-oh, what's gone wrong for ye since yesterday? You're wearing faces that would sour the cream."

"Someone broke into our cottage," said Emily.

Dad told her what had happened, but not what the thieves were looking for.

"Dreadful!" said Stella. "Makes one feel degraded

somehow, doesn't it?" She patted Emily's hand. "Can I get ye anything?"

"A bottle of water would be good," Emily said.

Dad ordered coffee.

"Sorry you had a spot of trouble," Angus said. "Luckily the thieves went away empty-handed."

"Yes," said Dad.

"Any idea what they were after?" Angus continued, warming to the topic. "After all, you had some valuable equipment, what with your laptop and cameras out in the open."

"Yes. That's what's so odd. They didn't take any of it."

Dad's cell phone rang. He went outside to answer it. When he returned, he stood beside Emily as if trying to decide something.

"What?" she asked. He looked away and back at her again. This must be serious. Had something happened to Mom?

He cleared his throat. "Em, one of my colleagues has asked if I could go to a local geological dig site, uh, this afternoon. They have no problem with you coming along."

"You're kidding, right?" She looked at him in disbelief, her dread turning to anger. "This is our holiday time."

"I know, Emily, but you might enjoy the site we're going to." He had that pleading look in his eyes again.

Emily slid off the stool. "This is supposed to be our

time together." She marched stiffly across the room and out the door, fighting back tears.

"Em, wait," Dad called after her, but she ignored him.

When she reached the street, tears blurred her eyes, but she made her way to a wooden bench a few metres along the street and sat down. Didn't her dad want to spend more time with her? How could he possibly think she'd enjoy standing around watching him work at a boring dig site?

Taking several deep breaths, she pulled a tissue out of her backpack and swiped at her eyes, then blew her nose. Somehow she had to go back inside and face everyone. Fine, if he didn't want her around, she'd stay behind at the cottage. Her decision made, she strode back into the pub and up to Dad.

"You go ahead this afternoon," she said stiffly. "I'd rather stay at the cottage and work on figuring things out with my research."

"But I'll be gone most of the afternoon. And I don't think it's such a good idea to leave you there after the break-in."

"I'll be fine, Dad," she said, ignoring Angus, who snuck a quick glance her way. "I'll be safe with Mrs. Kerns and the police and neighbours keeping an eye on the cottage. Even safer than before." She was glad she hadn't told him about being scared at the cemetery.

He seemed to waver.

"Besides, as you said before, I can get lots done, upload my photographs, draw my family charts. So I'll be ready for tomorrow. And I have a book to read. I'll be fine."

"As long as you stay in the cottage." Dad started to say something else, but was interrupted by a booming Scottish voice.

"Good afternoon, everyone."

Murdoch Lowry removed his tam as he entered the pub and lumbered across the floor, his kilt swishing against his legs. He seated himself on a stool near Emily and her dad, and plunked some coins onto the counter.

"Usual please, Stella," he said, and turned back to the pair of them.

"Just the person I want to see," said Emily, deliberately ignoring Dad.

"And what can I do for you today?"

Emily moved over beside him and plopped her notebook open. "Three things. First, I've been at the cemetery looking for ancestors and I've found a few, but I'm stuck."

"Specific family history and who's related to whom, I'm not verrrry good on," he said. "I'm more conversant with the political history and historical sites."

Emily looked disappointed.

"Wait now." He scratched his beard. "Stella. You've got some Robertson blood in you somewhere, don't you?"

Stella laughed, heading down the bar to them. "Aye,

and I'm related to Harry, too, in a roundaboot way, though he'd never want to admit it."

"Ergo, you have some Elliott connections."

She shrugged. "I've never thought much aboot our family history."

"Emily's talked to Harry Starke," Dad said, "but he doesn't seem to know too much, though there's definitely a family connection."

"Harry Starke's grandmother probably knows more," Emily said, "but I think he's holding back for some reason."

Then it hit her. If he knew more about the history than he was letting on, maybe he knew about the mirror, too. Could he have been the one to break in? Now, more than ever, she had to see his grandmother and find out what she knew.

"Do you happen to know where Harry's grandmother is, then?" Murdoch asked Stella.

"Aye, I do. She's across the village in the old geriatric centre. Mind, she's very frail, from what I understand."

"Go have a wee visit with her," Murdoch advised Emily. "I'll tell you how to get there."

"Ooh, Harry Starke won't like that." Stella's eyes twinkled.

"What he doesn't hear won't hurt him," Murdoch retorted. He took a big swig of his drink.

"I'm not so sure we should be going behind his back," said Dad. "It doesn't seem right."

Emily looked at her dad in surprise. "What harm can it do to go for a visit?"

Dad said, "It just seems a little dishonest to go behind his back."

"Couldn't we at least try?" said Emily, recklessly. "She doesn't have to see us when we get there."

"Emily's right," said Stella. "She can always refuse to see you."

"I suppose," said Dad, though Emily could see he wasn't happy about it.

Emily ignored him, not wanting to miss the opportunity or the adventure. He could be so staid sometimes, and he'd already proved he wasn't much interested in what she wanted to do.

"Do you know what would be a good time to visit?" she asked Stella.

"Probably best on an early morning. The poor dears are brighter at that time and not likely to be napping," said Stella, heading to the other end to serve another customer.

"We could go tomorrow," said Emily, referring to their previous agreement.

Dad twisted in his seat and looked sternly at Emily. "I still don't think we should just show up. How about we phone ahead and ask?"

"Okay," said Emily, shrugging. As long as she had a chance of talking to the woman, she was happy.

"Now that that's settled," Murdoch Lowry said, "how else can I be of assistance to you?"

"I was wondering where your family members are buried," she said, all of a sudden shy about asking about his family. "I'm curious about Kiresz from the painting and some of the others."

"No harm in asking," he said, sensing her discomfort. "They are mostly in the second row along the pathway leading up to the kirk. The oldest members, of course, are buried *in* St. Mary's Kirk, as they helped finance the building of it."

"So I could find Kiresz there?"

"Yes, she's honoured inside. You'll find the memorial stone on the floor just past the nave in the south transept."

Emily looked at him blankly, not having any idea where he meant.

Angus winked at her. "Just past the pews at the front, on the right-hand side."

"Thanks," she smiled at him. Maybe he wasn't so shallow after all. At least he was nice to her. And now that she knew where to find the information, she could make a quick trip back to the kirk any time to fill in all the names and dates.

"I have one more question for you," Emily said.

"Fire away."

"Can you tell me more about the Battle of Aikey Brae?" He'd tried to tell her on the hill when they first met, but she hadn't been interested enough then, thinking it wasn't important.

"Certainly. Especially now that I know more than I did before, having read up on it since then. What would you like to know?"

"Did the Bruces have a coat of arms?"

Emily waited while Murdoch thought about it.

"I believe it was a blue lion on a white background at that time, though it changed over the years."

"Like this?" Emily pulled her notebook out and flipped to her drawing.

"Why, yes!" He looked stunned. "How did you...?" Then he smiled. "Never mind, I've seen your powers at work before."

At last, she had some confirmation that the visions she'd been seeing were from the Battle of Aikey Brae.

"What did you say?" Dad asked. "Emily has some kind of powers?"

"An uncanny knack for knowing things," said Murdoch.

Emily was glad Murdoch hadn't given her away. He passed the notebook over to her dad.

"She's always had quite the imagination," said Dad, looking at the diagram and passing it back.

Emily passed it to Angus Peters, who was trying to peer at it from down the bar.

"So what happened after the Bruces won?" asked Emily, hoping for a clue to help her look for Larianna and her daughter.

Murdoch turned more serious. "The aftermath was

even more brutal than the battle. The Bruces wanted to ensure that no one who'd been loyal to the Earl of Buchan would rise up against them again. Their army destroyed all the castles and strongholds, and savagely murdered everyone in the vicinity, destroying their homes, farms and crops and slaughtering their cattle. It was a horrible massacre. Nothing and no one was spared."

Everyone fell silent.

Emily felt tears spring to her eyes. She took a long gulp of her water and set the glass back on the counter. No wonder Larianna had been distraught and angry. She'd lost everything, including her husband, her life and her baby during the Battle of Aikey Brae. What a horrible end!

"That's quite a dreadful story," said Dad.

"And unfortunately it's true," said Murdoch.

Somehow Larianna must have been separated from her baby or died before she knew what happened to her. She was stuck in time searching for her baby and would have no peace until she found her. But so much time had passed, why did it matter anymore?

"Here's something that may cheer you up," Murdoch said, reaching inside his tam for a sheet of folded paper.

"An old map," he said, spreading it on the counter. "And here is where your great-grandfather's croft was located." He pointed to a spot a couple of hundred metres to the west of the Scroghill Farm buildings. "It's still there and someone is living in it."

A wave of pleasure lit up Emily's face. It *was* the place she had been so drawn to, the one she'd taken photographs of when she'd made her dad stop the car on the way to Scroghill. The house with two chimneys.

"How wonderful." She passed it to her dad, who seemed pleased for her. "Thanks for finding it for me."

"I'll get a photocopy of it for you."

"That would be wonderful!"

He retrieved the map and folded it away again.

Angus watched until Murdoch looked up at him. The look they exchanged made Emily wonder what was going on between them.

"Do you think I could tour the place before I leave?"

"I thought you'd ask that, but I'm afraid the owners are away and a tour isn't possible," Murdoch said.

Disappointed, Emily thanked him for his efforts, then added, "At least I know where my ancestors lived."

"Guess we'd better get going," said Dad. "I have to meet the group in half an hour."

Emily sighed and said her goodbyes to the others remaining in the pub.

CHAPTER THIRTEEN

After Dad dropped her at the cottage, Emily worked in her journal. She organized the names she'd found in the cemetery, including Harry Starke's forebears, and began a family chart.

She came across a surprising discovery about the Starke family – a husband and wife who had died on the same day in 1956, both at young ages. She hadn't noticed the dates when she'd taken the photographs, because she'd been in such a hurry, but they were the right ages to be Harry's parents. This might explain why he never referred to them and maybe why he seemed so standoffish and prickly. She felt a twinge of sympathy for him, but that still didn't excuse breaking into the cottage to steal the mirror.

Studying the names and dates of the Elliott families, she discovered she didn't have any of their middle names, which probably would help her search the family farther back. If only she could speak to Harry Starke's grandmother.

Emily sat bolt upright. Why couldn't she? After all, Mrs. Starke lived in the same village – only a short distance away. She could call ahead, just as Dad insisted. She could go on her own.

Emily marched into the kitchen, found the telephone book and called the nursing home. She relayed her request and had to wait for a return call, which she answered on the first ring five minutes later.

"Mrs. Starke would be delighted to see you," said a young woman's voice. "She's quite anxious to meet you. Can you possibly come this afternoon?"

"I'd love to. I can be there in fifteen minutes."

Emily scurried around collecting her papers, stuffing them, her notebook and the mirror in her backpack, and headed out the door.

"RIGHT THIS WAY, PLEASE," said an assistant in a pale yellow uniform. "Mrs. Starke is waiting for you in the visitor's room."

Emily entered a carpeted room with armchairs covered in colourful flower prints. A woman with sparse grey hair sat in a wheelchair in the warmth and light of an open window.

Her green eyes popped open when Emily arrived.

"Hello," said Mrs. Starke.

Emily introduced herself.

"Thank you for coming." Mrs. Starke pulled her gnarled hands out from under the blanket draped over her lap and legs, and shook Emily's hand.

Emily had to strain to make out her thick Scots accent. She pulled up a chair close to the old lady's.

"So you belong to the Elliott family from Canada." Mrs. Starke looked long and hard at Emily.

"Yes. I was hoping you could tell me about the Elliotts that stayed *here.*"

"That's what Harry told me." The woman picked up a folded brown-edged paper from a nearby table. She handed it to Emily.

Emily unfolded the well-creased sheet to its full length, spreading it across her lap. She studied the lightly pencilled writing for a few moments. Although difficult to read, it was the Elliott family tree back to the 1700s. Everything she needed to fill in the blanks of her own family tree was right there in front of her, including the full names of her relatives who'd left for Canada. Someone had kept in touch with them after all, for a while at least.

"May I copy it?" she asked, reaching for her journal.

"You may have it," said the elderly lady with a wave of her hand. "My grandson isn't interested, and he's all the family I have. When I'm gone it will be tossed out."

"But surely Harry would want to keep it. It's part of his family, too."

Elizabeth Starke shook her head sadly. "He's more interested in things that have some cash value to them. Names on an old piece of paper aren't important to him. I raised him, I know."

"How sad," said Emily.

"I know what you're thinking, and you're right. He's a little rough around the edges," the old lady chuckled. "You go on now, quinie – take the chart."

"Thank you so much." Emily could hardly believe her luck. "I will cherish it."

"I know you will. Anyone who comes such a long distance to find their ancestors surely has strong family values, and I approve of that."

Emily folded the oversized sheet back up and tucked it in her backpack. Now, did she dare ask the question that was most important to her? She couldn't miss the chance.

"I know about the split in the family between Alexander and George, and that George, being the younger brother, needed to find work at another estate. But do you know any other reason why the family never had much contact after that time, especially after they went to Canada?"

Mrs. Starke gazed into the distance, lost in thought. Emily thought she wasn't going to answer, but finally she stirred.

"It was all so long ago. There seems no reason to keep it secret any more. I don't suppose *it* even exists anymore, if it ever did."

Emily's pulse quickened. What was the secret? What did Mrs. Starke mean by *it?*

"It's daft really," the old lady said. "Some dispute over a mirror, if you can believe it."

Emily leaned in closer. "A mirror?"

"The story goes that it was a fancy looking glass with precious gems in the handle or something. It was worth a great deal of money and the family could have sold it and been fairly well off. It had been handed down through the generations until it came to George's wife."

"Not Alexander's wife?" asked Emily. "I thought things were traditionally handed down to the oldest in a family."

"They generally are, but this was something special that was passed down to George's wife by her mother or grandmother. It was said to have special powers for telling the future and was gifted only to those who could use it."

She cackled. "We Scots are great ones for believing in the second sight, though I don't rightly understand it."

She continued after a moment. "Alexander Elliott wanted his brother to convince his wife to sell the mirror and help them all out, but they refused. And rightly so. There are some things in this world more precious than money. I don't even know how Alexander came to know about it, or why he thought it should be used to help his family, when it was George's family that was the most destitute of them all."

She sat silent for a moment, lost in memories. "He was a bad apple that one – always causing trouble for the family and himself. Lost his position once, but finally landed on his feet."

"What do you mean?" asked Emily, eager to hear what might have happened to the wayward Alexander.

"He became a little too big for his boots on their farm at Skillymarno, but managed to connive his way into working on another estate. Good thing, too, as his reputation was beginning to be known and he soon would have had to leave the area entirely."

Emily brought the conversation back to the mirror. "Do you know where the mirror came from in the beginning?" She might be able to fill in the gap between Mairead's legend and the mirror coming into the Elliott family.

Mrs. Starke shook her head. "No. It was said that those who had the mirror and were able to use it properly could see the lineage of the person to pass it on to. But as I say, I don't even know if it exists. It was only a story when I was a wee girl, you understand."

Emily had to know without delay. "Have you told this story to Harry?"

"Oh yes. He liked to hear the old stories, though I didn't tell him that one until a few days ago."

So now Emily knew why Harry had been reluctant to let Emily meet his grandmother. Why he wouldn't answer questions, or pretended not to know things. He'd wanted to get the mirror for himself. A surge of anger swept over Emily, but then she calmed down.

"My Harry seemed keen on the story. I can't surprise him with much these days, but that one certainly caught his interest." The old lady smiled. "Of course that mirror would be beyond value today. But it's only a story, you know. I wouldn't put any store in it at all."

Emily suppressed a giggle. Wouldn't Mrs. Starke be surprised if she knew that very mirror was in the backpack sitting at her feet? She let the moment pass.

Mrs. Starke was starting to droop in her chair, her eyes attempting to close.

"I think I'd better go now," said Emily. "You look tired."

She grasped the old woman's knobbly hands in hers.

"Thank you for allowing me to visit, and for sharing your stories and the family chart with me."

"You're most welcome. I have enjoyed myself very much. You're a nice wee lass, not like Harry said at all. He keeps things from me, you know... He thinks he's protecting me, but not much can harm an old lady like me anymore."

Outside, Emily shook off her irritation at Harry and almost skipped away. She had found out even more about her ancestors than she'd dared hope for. Mairead had said Emily would come to know a different family than the one she sought. Her search was taking her beyond the Elliotts – way beyond.

How did Mairead know the history of the mirror? And why was there such urgency for Emily to find the answers?

She had to see Mairead again.

CHAPTER FOURTEEN

As Emily rounded the corner back to Nicholls Cottage, she saw Dad standing at the front step waiting for her. She waved.

"You'll never guess what I have," she called out.

When she got closer, she saw anger etched in his face.

"Emily Marie Bradford, where have you been?" he demanded angrily. "The deal was you were going to stay in the cottage where you'd be safe."

"But I was fine," she answered, as the blood pounded in her eardrums. She was in for it now. Did she admit where she'd gone? Might as well get it over with.

"I went to see Mrs. Starke. I was only a few blocks away."

"You left the cottage and went to Mrs. Starke's without my knowledge? I thought we agreed we wouldn't intrude on her." He glared as she went past him up the steps.

"We agreed we wouldn't go without calling first, and I did. She wanted me to come right away." Emily set her backpack on a chair and pulled out the folded chart.

"See what she gave me." Emily opened the chart and laid it on the table.

He ran his fingers through his hair and turned away from her. She'd never seen her dad so angry.

"Don't you ever do something like that again," he warned. "Especially without telling anyone where you're going."

"Sorry, Dad," she said quietly.

"You could have called me on my cell phone, or waited until I got back."

"I didn't think about it. I was just so excited at finally being able to connect with Mrs. Starke." Truthfully, the idea to let him know had never entered her mind. "I didn't expect you'd be back this early."

"I didn't expect to be back this early either, but that's beside the point," he said.

"I knew I would be safe. It's broad daylight."

"You could have at least told Peggy Kerns where you were going." He didn't seem to be able to stop reprimanding her. "She was worried when I said you were gone."

"I said I'm sorry, Dad. I was just trying to get as much work done as possible, just like you do all the time," she answered a little sarcastically. She knew she was making things worse for herself, but she couldn't help it.

Dad looked at her, stunned.

The words kept pouring out of her mouth, like a gushing volcano pent up for too long.

"Well it's true. You fall asleep all the time, because you're obviously exhausted from working all the time. You never relax even though we're supposed to be on holiday. I'm just doing what you do."

Dad blew out a long breath. "Go over and tell Mrs. Kerns you're okay, while I put away my gear."

Emily rallied herself and skirted past him, but he reached out for her and hugged her.

"You had me worried sick," he said. "Emily, if something bad happened to you, I don't know what I'd do."

She hugged him back tightly. "I promise I won't do it again." At least now she knew he cared. He was still her dad, and he still loved her.

"And I'll try to relax more," he said.

By the time Emily came back from letting Peggy Kerns know she was okay and apologizing for making her worry, Dad had calmed down and was looking at the family chart.

"I'm glad you found so much information, Em," he said. "We still have a little time in the day yet. Is there anywhere you want to go?"

"I'd like to visit Mairead again," she said without hesitation.

"I meant in the village. Let's save the visit to the laird's place for tomorrow."

"Uh, okay, how about we go to St. Mary's and look for the monuments and plaques in the kirk for Murdoch's ancestors?"

Dad nodded.

On the walk over, he asked how her visit had gone with Mrs. Starke. Emily described the encounter almost word for word.

At the end she said, "I bet Harry Starke didn't even ask her if I could visit. And he knows about the mirror, too. Do you think he tried to steal it? Mrs. Starke said she told him about it *a few days ago.*"

"We don't really know that's what the thief wanted."

"I don't think there's any doubt," she answered.

"There may be others to consider," he said. "We haven't exactly been quiet about what we're doing in the area. Murdoch knows. And there's his housekeeper, and Ian McPhee, too."

"Oh, it couldn't be Mairead," Emily began. But she realized she hadn't known any of these people for long. And there were always people in the pub. But Harry Starke kept coming to mind.

She recalled how Harry Starke had watched her that day in the cemetery, and his efforts to keep her away from his grandmother. Ian McPhee seemed very unlikely. Murdoch Lowry had helped a great deal, and she couldn't picture Mairead picking locks. Angus Peters had given them helpful tips, too.

Emily wanted to look at the stones and memorials

for Murdoch's family. She left Dad at the edge of the cemetery, examining interesting inscriptions.

On one side of the uneven stone walkway that led to the door of St. Mary's, tall tombstones leaned towards her as if ready to topple over. The flat stones on the other side had sunk so far into the earth that their engraved surfaces were below the level of the grass.

She scanned the second rows of both sides and found a couple of women called Kiresz. She photographed them for her records, but their dates were more recent than those for the Kiresz from the painting.

The metal latch creaked as she opened the heavy oak door. She had to use her full body weight to push it inwards. She entered the silence and gloom and began studying the engraved plates on the floor. Within moments she found what she was looking for.

Kiresz Sangster Lowry – 1787–1875.

This had to be the Kiresz from the painting! Was she connected to Margaret Elsbeth Elliott, Emily's great-grandmother, who had also been a Sangster?

Emily studied the engraving in greater detail and took pictures. It was more important than ever that she see Murdoch and Mairead again as soon as possible.

She and Dad walked back to the cottage in amicable silence. When they returned, Dad immediately drew out his laptop and set it up. He seemed to have forgotten her presence again.

"I'm going up to my room," Emily said.

"Um-hmm," Dad mumbled, sifting through his papers.

Emily exhaled noisily. "Then I'm going to climb out my window and jump off the roof."

"That's good," he said, typing something into the laptop.

Tears sprang into her eyes. He hadn't even noticed what she'd said.

She picked up her backpack, and dragged herself upstairs. What did she have to do to get his attention?

Oh well, she had her own work to do. She settled in and worked diligently for a long while, note-taking and drawing family diagrams, but she still had so many questions. And they were only in the area for another couple of days.

A sudden wave of tiredness swept over her and all she wanted to do was sleep. Moments later, she snuggled against a pillow and was halfway through a thought about the family connections when her mind shut down.

She jerked awake and looked at the clock. Whew! She'd only been asleep for a half-hour. Time to see if Murdoch was in the pub so she could confirm the information she'd found in the kirk.

She stomped a little going down the stairs, hoping Dad would notice her and stop working. She wanted him to go with her. But he wasn't at the dining room table working at his laptop. She found him in the sunroom, stretching and yawning after his own nap.

"I see you're hard at work!" she teased.

"I didn't mean to go to sleep. I guess, you're right. I'm more tired than I realized," Dad said, rising. Papers fluttered to the floor.

Emily scrambled to help pick them up. They almost bonked heads, which made them chuckle.

"Ready to do something?" he asked.

"Sure. It's time to go to the pub," she said, pleased that Dad was in a good mood now. "I thought we could go to there for supper. I need more information."

"Fine and dandy," said Dad.

Emily laughed. "Where did you get that saying from?"

"I don't recall. Why?"

"It sounds so old-fashioned."

"I suppose it is," Dad said with a silly grin. "So let's shake a leg, get our butts in gear..."

"Let's pretend we're going to a fire," said Emily.

"We can be there better late than never..." Dad said with a little sparkle in his eye.

"Let's make sure not to put Harry Starke's nose out of joint." Emily pulled her backpack on.

Dad helped settle the straps across her shoulders. "Yes, he seems to have a chip on his shoulder."

"Yes, I've seen the writing on the wall," Emily joked. "But maybe his bark is worse than his bite."

"It could be a blessing in disguise."

"Or he has an axe to grind." She kept the idioms

going. She couldn't remember having this much fun with her dad.

"Or maybe we're barking up the wrong tree."

They laughed and joked all the way down the street. Emily hadn't seen her dad laugh like that for a very long time. Maybe things would be okay between them, after all.

By the time they arrived at the pub, Emily was doubled over with laughter. They must have come up with thirty or more sayings, stretching to make them all fit the circumstances.

"Why are you two so cheery?" asked Stella, grinning.

"Your guess is as good as mine." Emily quipped one last saying, as she climbed up on the stool, which set Dad to laughing again. They explained the game they'd been playing. Soon they had Stella laughing too.

Harry Starke strode into the pub. "I have a bone to pick with you, Emily Bradford."

If Emily hadn't burst into another gale of laughter at that moment, she might have been frightened by his manner, even worried that he might have found out about her visit to his mother. But Dad and Stella were laughing so hard, and she could barely catch her breath.

The outrage on Harry Starke's face made them laugh even harder.

"A picture paints a thousand words," Stella howled, and asked him for his order.

"I don't think I'll have anything. I didn't come to be made fun of." He turned on his heels and started back towards the door.

"Wait," Emily called after him. "We're sorry. We were in the middle of a private joke."

He stopped and looked at them.

Stella waved him back. Dad was still grinning, but had composed himself. Emily swallowed hard to keep from breaking into laughter again.

"We weren't making fun of you. Honest." Stella patted the bar, and held up an empty glass, inviting his order.

"We were reeling off old sayings," she said by way of explanation.

"All right, then." Harry returned but took a stool further down the bar.

"My, uh, usual," he said to Stella.

She brought his order, and disappeared into the kitchen. They could hear her chuckling somewhere in the back. Emily tried to mask the sound.

"So what was it you wanted to say to me?" she asked. "Nothing serious, I hope?"

"Certainly it's serious. People saying I haven't cooperated in helping you. When that's not the case at all."

"I've never said anything of the kind." She'd thought it, but never said it to anyone.

"Nor I," said Dad.

"It's certainly come back to me."

"If the shoe fits, wear it," said Murdoch Lowry, joining them as if on cue. "If it doesn't, don't worry about it."

It was all Emily could do not to crack a smile. She didn't dare look at her dad.

Harry Sharpe's faced turned a bright shade of pink. "Of course it's not true. I've told them everything I know."

Except you knew about the mirror, Emily thought.

"Great, then there's no problem," said Murdoch, taking a stool next to Emily. "So, quinie, what have you been up to all day?"

She omitted the visit to Mrs. Starke, but relayed everything that she'd found at the kirk. She asked him about Kiresz's middle name of Sangster.

Murdoch looked dumbfounded for a moment. "I've never studied our own family beyond the male lineage."

"Really?"

He laughed. "And lately, I've been studying records about your Elliotts and Scroghill. Time I looked into my own." He patted her hand. "I do remember the Sangster name, of course."

Emily explained about the Sangster name in her family tree. She wished she could tell him about Mrs. Starke giving her the chart, but Harry Starke still sat only a short distance away.

"Seems we may be distantly related, too." Murdoch seemed pleased. "I'll see what else I can find at home, though I don't recall anyone in the family taking a particular interest in anyone beyond the Lowrys."

"Family researching is huge," said Emily. "You end up going through different branches than the one you started out with."

Again, she recalled Mairead's words about finding a different family from the one she was looking for.

CHAPTER FIFTEEN

The next morning, Emily grabbed an apple from the ceramic bowl on the counter and took a large bite. As she passed the mirror in the front hall, she noticed her tangled hair. Holding the apple in her mouth, she grabbed a hairbrush and swept it through her hair.

A sudden knock on the door startled her.

She whirled around to find Peggy Kerns, giving her an amused look through the window in the front door.

"Trying the ancient ritual, I see?" she said, as she entered.

"Pardon?" Emily said.

"Eating an apple in front of a mirror while combing your hair will conjure your true love's image in the mirror."

"I've never heard that before." Emily took a quick glance into the mirror.

Peggy Kerns chuckled. "Aye, you may not have

intended it, quinie, but that's what you were conjuring up all the same."

Emily shrugged and smiled. "I guess it doesn't work for me."

"Never mind, it will come to you all in good time." She peered around the corner into the kitchen.

"Can I help you with anything?"

"Aye, I was wondering how you were gettin' on since the break-in, and if you'd be needin' anything."

"I think we have everything, but I'll tell my dad you stopped by."

Peggy turned to go.

"I guess there's no word on who might have done it?" Emily asked.

Peggy Kerns shook her head.

They chatted a moment, reviewing the sequence of events. Peggy Kerns ended by saying, "The only person who went by that morning was Angus Peters."

"Angus Peters? But I thought you said no one had gone by."

"I thought you asked about anyone suspicious. Angus goes by every day. Well, I'd best be off. Cheerio." Peggy Kerns sailed out the door, her red curls bouncing on her shoulders.

Emily mentally went through the list of suspects again and moved Angus higher up the list, even though she didn't want to believe it. She added Peggy Kerns way down at the bottom of the list under the "probably nots," where she'd placed Ian McPhee and a few others. Harry Starke was still at the top of her list! Had she missed anyone?

LATER THAT MORNING, Emily marched up Laird Elgivin's sweeping front steps toting her backpack and pressed the doorbell. She was preparing to ask for Mairead, when the heavy oak door swung open, and there she was.

"Good morning, quinie. You've timed it perfectly. Laird Elgivin has just gone off for his morning walk. Come in, and we'll have some tea."

Emily was not overly surprised that Mairead had known she'd come to see her. This was just another in a long sequence of strange things happening to her.

Mairead noticed Emily's dad sitting in the car. "Would your father like to join us?"

Emily shook her head. "He's busy reading some papers for work. Though I won't stay too long."

Mairead led the way to the kitchen, filled with the aroma of baking bread and almonds and another smell she couldn't identify. Caramel?

"I'm sure you'll have time for some of my sticky toffee pudding?" Mairead turned to her with a twinkle in her eyes. The kettle was already whistling.

"I won't pass that up," said Emily. She remembered Murdoch telling her how good it was.

"Seat yourself at the table, and I'll bring you some."

Mairead bustled about the kitchen preparing tea and scooping a healthy helping of the pudding into a bowl. Setting everything in front of Emily on the large oak table, she poured the tea and sat across from her.

"Ah, you are looking better already." Mairead smiled.

Emily looked perplexed.

"When you first arrived you were so serious and worried. Now you are relaxing. You have something exciting to tell me, and you need explanations. You are very close to knowing what you need to know about the mirror's lineage."

Emily nodded, no longer surprised by Mairead's deductions. She stirred some sugar and milk into her tea, and sampled the pudding. The sweet concoction melted in her mouth.

"Mmmm." Emily closed her eyes.

Mairead grinned with pleasure.

"Would I be able to get the recipe for this?" Emily asked, shyly.

Even more pleased, Mairead immediately drew out a sheet of paper with some kind of drawing on the top from a kitchen drawer and jotted down the ingredients. "Mind, I don't really measure anything exact, but with practice, I'm sure you'll do well."

"I doubt it will ever turn out as well as yours," said Emily, "but having the recipe will also be a good keepsake."

Mairead gave her a hug and handed the sheet to Emily. She tucked it into her backpack.

"Now, to answer your questions." Mairead looked into the distance to some far-off place. Emily didn't even have to ask her questions. Mairead knew.

"The mirror, as you've likely guessed, was handed down through the maternal line of your ancestors, and not always through the eldest. It could be any female in the family who had the gift of being fey, and sometimes there was more than one daughter with the second sight."

"How could they tell who to give it to then, if there was a choice?"

"That was determined by whichever one was drawn to the mirror, just as you were. The women who care for the mirror always know who the next in line will be. By the way, being fey is not exclusive to women. Men can possess the gift, too, but this mirror, even though it was made by a male, was given to a special woman and passed down only through the female line and finally came to you."

"But that's a fluke," said Emily. "I only happened to find it."

Mairead raised an eyebrow. "You were meant to find it. Never doubt that you are the intended owner."

"But what about my grandmother? I don't think she ever used it. She never told me about it before she died."

"Some who are given the second sight have no need or desire to use the mirror. But she also knew you'd find it, if you were meant to have it."

Emily let the words sink in as she ate another mouthful of pudding.

"And you do know how to use it, but you let doubt get in your way. You don't need to try so hard."

Emily relaxed physically after that, though her mind still whirled with unanswered questions. "Was that why I couldn't get anything more last night?"

"Could also be there wasn't anything more to impart."

Emily realized that Larianna's knowledge of her physical world had ended at her death. She'd had no more information to give.

"How do *you* know the history of the mirror?"

Mairead spoke simply. "We are of the same family."

"You're part of the Elliott family, too?"

Mairead grinned. "No, but we do descend from Kiresz's line."

"But then, you should have the mirror," sputtered Emily.

"No, quinie, I said *we*, not I. It was bestowed in the right manner. Besides, I've never had any children, so it would have stopped with me."

"Wait, what did you mean that *we* are descendants of Kiresz's? How?"

"We both come from her line, but in slightly different ways."

While Emily thought that over, Mairead continued. "I come from the line of women that are keepers of the legend. We make sure that the story will not be lost until the new owner comes into possession and comes to understand the mirror's ways."

"Do you know how we're connected?" asked Emily. She didn't even know Mairead's last name.

"I only know my direct family members with any certainty."

Emily pulled out the chart and spread it on the table. She told Mairead how she'd come to have it.

Mairead studied the information and started to laugh.

"See here, Emily, my great-grandmother and your great-great-grandmother were sisters. We're more related than I knew!"

Emily laughed. "I'm glad," she said.

"Me too," said Mairead, pressing Emily's hand in both of hers.

"I wonder if we could trace this any further back?" asked Emily eager to find out more.

Mairead chuckled. "Maybe with some serious digging, though the official records don't go much beyond this. If I ever find anything more, I will be sure to relay it to you."

"Thanks. And I'll make copies of this for you," Emily offered in return.

"Wonderful, quinie!"

Emily turned to her most important question. "So what is the urgency for me to know about the mirror and to find the first Kiresz?"

Mairead took a deep breath. "Two things. For one, as I mentioned, my line ends with me, and all others that could possibly tell you anything about your family are elderly, as you have no doubt realized. Any of the people who could help you fill in the story will soon be gone from this world. The old ways are dying out."

Emily gulped. "You mean everything about the mirror will be up to me from then on? I'll have to keep the mirror and the legend, too?"

Mairead nodded and smiled.

"And your daughters, for you will surely have two."

Wide-eyed, Emily gawked at the older woman. Her teacup rattled on the saucer as she set it down.

"But maybe it belongs to Laird Elgivin's family instead? His ancestors obviously come from the same line."

Mairead laughed out loud. "You can't get away from your responsibility that easily."

"I don't think that's so far-fetched," said Emily, a little miffed. "I mean, the portrait of Kiresz looks similar to the original woman in the mirror. It's obvious that the two families are related."

Mairead snorted, "That's all it means – that they are related, not that they deserve to have the mirror."

"But I don't understand the connection between them, your family, and the Elliotts. Laird Elgivin's family was clearly a wealthy landowning family, but your ancestors seemed to be their servants and mine were poor crofters."

"It hasn't always been that way," Mairead explained. "Although there were distinct social rules about the gentry not marrying beneath them, some actually did. There were not always arranged marriages in the upper classes. Some even married for love." She smiled. "Like Kiresz's marriage into Laird Elgivin's family. Aristocrats and members from your common family and mine probably married, as well."

"They would have known about the mirror, too?" Emily asked.

"Yes, those who were either owners of the mirror or keepers of the story."

"Would the current Laird Elgivin know the story?" Emily instantly had a terrible thought. What if he had tried to steal the mirror?

"Possibly, though I've never told it to him."

Surely Laird Elgivin, who owned such a beautiful place, wouldn't steal the mirror for the money. But hadn't he said that rich landowners were rich only in property and not in available cash?

"So how many people know about it?"

"Only those that need to, although sometimes an extra person or two discovers the secret."

Mairead shook her head. "It's not who you want it to be, quinie."

"You know about the break-in?"

Mairead cackled. "Yes, but only because Laird Elgivin told me."

"So Harry Starke didn't do it?" Emily asked with an edge to her voice.

Mairead shook her head again.

"But who else is there?"

"Remember that in villages like this, with few outsiders moving in, almost everyone is related or they are familiar with families who are related in some way."

Lost in thought, Emily went over everything she'd learned, and all the people she'd met. Any of them could have known the story.

And then, she knew.

"Angus Peters."

Mairead nodded. "Yes, you are right."

He'd been curious about the interior of their cottage and had fiddled with the doorknob when he stopped to visit. He even knew about Dad's laptop and camera equipment sitting in the dining room, but he'd never stepped far enough inside to see where they were. And he knew nothing had been taken before he was told. Peggy Kerns had seen him that morning, too. And he knew they were out. He'd seen them at the Abbey of Deer and knew he had time before they returned.

But what motive did he have to steal it?

The word *greed* came unbidden to her mind.

"He's a greedy young fellow," Mairead said.

How had he known about the mirror? Harry Starke had probably told him in order to impress him. Those two seemed to be involved in some kind of one-upmanship. But there had to be something more.

"He seems to have enough money and a nice car. Why would he do something like that?" Emily asked.

"He doesn't understand there are things in this world more precious than money. He's an out-and-out scallywag."

"I see." Emily remembered the long-unpaid bar tab.

"He's also never been one to hang on to any money, and I know he's always felt he was entitled to more than he has."

"I don't understand," said Emily.

"Angus Peters is a cousin of some sort to Laird Elgivin. And he has always resented that Murdoch Lowry inherited the entire estate, even though there was no question that it was done rightfully."

Emily had forgotten the use of middle names, but now she remembered one she'd seen. Andrew Lowry Peters. *Angus Peters* was related to Murdoch's family. He could have known about the mirror, too.

Mairead rose and began clearing the table, as Emily mulled over her feelings towards Angus.

"Always trust your instincts," Mairead added.

"But I don't want it to be him," Emily admitted.

"Why, because he was charming to you?"

Emily nodded.

"Pffft. There are appealing rogues everywhere, but mostly they are out for their own gain. A pretty face and compelling eyes don't a man make."

"There probably isn't any evidence to prove it was him," Emily said.

"Quite possibly not, but I hope he owns up to it, though he won't ever want to face the consequences." A little sadness crept into Mairead's voice.

"I guess some things aren't as they seem. Maybe that's why people say not to judge a book by its cover." Oh no, she was resorting to Dad's sayings.

Mairead agreed.

"What if someone else tries to take the mirror?" asked Emily, afraid of being the sole person responsible for protecting it.

"You own the mirror, and it is yours to keep. Although some may try, none will be able to steal it, and you are not in any danger, Emily."

"How do you know?"

Mairead grasped Emily's hands reassuringly.

"The mirror and its legend are handed down only through the direct line of those who are either its keepers or its guardians. You will always have strong messages to guide you in keeping the mirror safe when you need it. You did the day of the break-in, didn't you?"

"Yes," Emily replied, recalling the strong desire to take it with her to the Abbey of Deer. "But how does it all work?"

"The answers you seek will be revealed through the

mirror, all in good time. Before you leave Scotland, all that you need to know will be shown to you. And you will be happy to know your family, though it's not the one you sought."

Emily looked doubtfully at the older woman. That was twice she'd said Emily would know another family than the one she was researching, which had turned out true so far. And twice she'd said Emily would find out what she needed to know, but there wasn't much time... She only had one day left.

Mairead released Emily's hand, and smiled. "The outcome will be a positive experience. Accept what you are shown, and have fun learning about it. The mirror is to be used for good."

Another question popped into Emily's head. "How did you know for sure I had the mirror?"

"Come with me." Mairead led her through the back passageways to the painting of the mother and child.

Emily stood in front of the painting, awed again by the mesmerizing realness of it. Kiresz and her daughter seemed to be smiling intently back at her.

Mairead came softly up beside her. She held a vanity mirror at arm's length in front of Emily.

"Look at Kiresz and then look into the mirror."

Emily gazed at Kiresz in the painting, then at herself. She drew in a sharp breath.

"Now you see it, too," said Mairead. "You both have the same features, especially your eyes."

"You mean we could even be related?"

"Indeed, I'm sure of it!"

"Now compare yourself to the daughter. She's only slightly younger than you, and the resemblance might be even more noticeable."

Emily studied the young girl. "We have the same oval brown eyes, too," she said. The shape of their faces and colour of their hair also matched.

"Do you have your camera with you?" Mairead asked.

"Yes."

Mairead took photographs of Emily standing on a chair beside the painting so all of their faces would be close to the same height. After that, Emily took some of the whole painting.

Emily realized she didn't know the daughter's name.

"Emmarie," Mairead answered.

Emily wasn't surprised by the older woman knowing her question, but she was surprised by the answer.

"How strange. I had two special people in my life, one called Emma and my Grandmother Renfrew was Mary."

"Yes, I know," Mairead answered with a serene smile.

Emily stood a moment longer, saying a silent good-bye to both mother and daughter. She almost felt that they were smiling back at her.

Mairead led her to the front door.

Emily stopped. "Wait. You said there were two reasons for finding out what happened to Larianna's baby. What's the second?"

Mairead gave her a mysterious smile. "Hasn't Larianna been asking you to hurry?"

"Yes, but I don't understand why."

"My instinct tells me that she hasn't been able to connect as strongly with anyone else through the mirror as she has with you. She may feel you are her last hope of finding her bairn."

"But surely Larianna has found her child by now, even if she had to wait until Kiresz went through her whole life and eventually died."

"I can't answer to that," Mairead said. "It seems that Larianna has been wandering earthbound for all these centuries... I sense that her spirit will not rest until she knows what happened *in her own lifetime*."

Emily mulled this. "But I have only seen Larianna through the mirror, not her baby."

"Consult it again," advised Mairead.

Emily nodded, deep in thought. Maybe she could ask Kiresz to appear. It was worth a try.

She glanced down at the backpack near her feet. Mairead's eyes followed hers.

Emily reached a decision. She pulled the box from her backpack and set it on the hall table. Opening it, she brought out the mirror.

Mairead came to her side and gazed at the intricate

gemstones and filigree ivy metalwork.

"You can touch it or hold it if you like," offered Emily.

"No, dear, I would rather not, though 'tis lovely."

Emily turned it over and they looked into the glass.

Mairead touched Emily's wrist. "Best tuck it away and look at it on your own. 'Tis enough that I have seen it."

Emily obliged, silently.

"Your father is waiting."

"Yes, I'm sure he's run out of patience," said Emily with a brief smile.

She put the mirror away and clutched her backpack to her chest. The contents were more precious to her than ever.

"Thank you for everything," Emily said, as they stood at the front door and Emily put on her backpack.

"You are most welcome, dear heart. I know you will soon uncover the truth."

"Yes, I feel that, too," said Emily, and she truly did.

"Just remember, the mirror will give you the answers you seek."

Mairead wrapped her arms around Emily and they hugged for several moments. Emily felt the older woman's strength and knew they would have a strong bond for all time.

"*Dewlessa,*" said Mairead, with tears in her eyes.

"*Dewlessa,*" Emily said, knowing she'd never see Mairead in person again.

CHAPTER SIXTEEN

Dad was slumped over the steering wheel, fast asleep. He didn't stir until Emily clicked open the passenger door and slid inside.

"How'd it go?" he mumbled, clearing his throat and straightening up.

"Good," said Emily, feeling subdued but thankful for knowing Mairead. So much had happened in the last few days that her brain felt like soup whirled in a blender. She needed to find a place to think things through.

"Do you think we could swing by the Aikey Brae Stone Circle again?" she asked.

"Sure," said Dad, starting the car. "I wouldn't mind taking another look at the battle site, too."

They took the longer route to see the sights one last time, manoeuvring through Old Deer and Stuartfield. They swung past Scroghill Farm and the little croft where her great-grandparents had lived. Dad stopped so

Emily could take a last, lingering look, imprinting the image of the cozy stone house with the two chimneys in her mind. Before they drove on, Emily told her dad about her certainty that Angus Peters had been the thief, and why.

"Definitely sounds like he's the culprit," Dad said. "But we can't prove it."

"I know. He didn't actually take anything that we could catch him with." Emily felt the anger rising. He'd used her to get information for the break-in.

When they parked at the bottom of the Parkhouse Hill entrance, Emily reached for her backpack. She heard a fast car approaching around the curve, slammed the door and got out of the way.

"Speak of the devil," said Dad, as Angus Peter's lime-green MG appeared.

He showed no signs of slowing, but Emily stood in the road and waved him down. He stopped and rolled down his window as Emily approached.

He smiled and greeted her warmly.

"Don't give me any more of your phony smiles, Angus Peters. I'm sick of the way you stare at me all the time."

"What?" His mouth dropped open. "That's because you look like the woman in the painting. The one at Murdoch's house."

"Oh," Emily said. He'd noticed she looked like Kiresz. "So that's how you knew about the mirror!"

He tried to speak, but she stopped him. "I know you broke into our place. Don't try to deny it!"

"What if I did? You don't know what it's like for me!"

"I know you're a scallywag," Emily said. "So there!"

She whirled and returned to her stunned dad's side. "That was satisfying," said Emily, though her knees felt weak.

"Aye, you've got nothing on me, you silly pipsqueak," Angus yelled and roared away.

Dad hugged her and started laughing. "Now I know you can take care of yourself, like all the Elliott women."

Emily grinned. "He's not worth worrying about." She knew that to be true. He was bound to get into more trouble, and one day he'd pay for it.

She and Dad trundled uphill with the scent of roses and clover wafting from the hedges. Long grasses blew in the wind and whirring insects circled around them. Everything seemed similar to back home on the prairies. She could understand why her ancestors had chosen to settle where they did.

At the top, before they entered the pine forest, Emily stopped and surveyed the scene down the long, steep slope towards the Aikey Brae fairgrounds and battlefield. So much history had taken place on this very hillside, and it seemed to be connected to her. There must be something important about Larianna that still needed to be discovered; otherwise, why would she keep appearing in the mirror?

Dad had moved off to the side a little, occupied with his own thoughts. She had an idea.

"Dad, would you be okay with doing your own thing while I spend some time here by myself?" she asked with some authority.

Dad looked a little surprised. "Sure. I'll wander around and take some photographs. I'll meet you back here when you're done."

"Great!" She adjusted her backpack. "See you later."

As Dad headed off, Emily thought again about the last time she'd been here, and of Larianna's plea to help find her daughter. Where would she begin, and how would she travel back in time to look for Kiresz?

Something drew her along the path down the hillside. Following a deer trail, she made her way down the slope, stopping every once in a while to look around. If she could get a sense of where the last battle she'd seen in the mirror had been, she might find Larianna. She continued downwards for several metres, hearing whispered voices. They grew louder and her head felt light.

Moments later, Emily heard shouts. In an instant, she was in the middle of the fighting. Around her, men grunted and screamed as they fell. She leapt away as a club cracked down on a man's head beside her. Fighting was going on as far as she could see in every direction, on the hillside and down into the valley.

In terror, Emily looked for a place to hide. She ducked behind a tree, momentarily out of the way as two barbaric-looking swordsmen parried clumsily on the other side of a wide-girthed tree trunk. The moist smell of upturned earth and grass mixed with blood streaming from open wounds on men lying around her; young and old alike.

She moved to another tree as the clanking of swords came closer, only to find her way blocked by a horse, rearing as its rider speared a man attacking him from the ground. She watched in horror as two other men on foot reached for the rider and pulled him roughly to the ground, then beat him with clubs. Racing to a clump of bushes, she dived under them, willing no one to find her and hoping a horse wouldn't step on her.

With her dark hair wrapped in a ponytail, and wearing jeans, Emily didn't look like any of the women or village men around her, many of whom were dressed in peasant garb of coarse tunics and simple hose, with sticks as weapons. Few of them had much in the way of footwear or protective clothing.

The wealthier men and warriors, however, were properly outfitted with shields and helmets, forming ranks and listening to shouted orders. Arrows flew everywhere and she was scared to move, watching the scene in terror and bewilderment, and hoping to catch sight of Larianna among the chaos.

She noticed a small group of low, straw-roofed huts on the other side of a small rise. As she watched, women and children with bundles in their arms slipped out the back away, keeping low to the ground. Younger women helped the elderly and shielded the little children in the centre of the group. They seemed to be trying to make it to a thicket near the river, under cover of occasional bushes and the tight stands of trees that sparsely dotted the landscape.

Emily headed towards them, creeping behind trees or rocks when she could. When she saw an open space, she raced across the grass as fast she could go, hoping no one saw her. Everything was happening so fast. Emily didn't know where to look for Larianna, but following the women and children seemed a likely start.

Without warning, the huts were set upon by riders with burning torches. The roofs ignited and the fire leapt high, becoming a large blaze in moments. A smokey haze added to the confusion as the fighting continued. The men seemed to stagger and tire, yet they fought until they could no longer go on, dropping from fatigue and wounds, one after another.

The escaping group of women and children hurried faster, until one old woman fell to the ground. A young woman stopped, set her belongings down and struggled to help her, but the old woman encouraged her and the others to leave her and go on. When it was obvious the old woman couldn't stand and that she'd won a frenzied and heated argument between them, the younger one hugged her, then gathered her own bundle tightly in her arms and ran to catch up to the others.

Emily watched, with a fist in her mouth to hold back her screams, as a group of warriors on horseback pursued the escaping group. The young woman who had tried to help the older one managed to break away, racing for some nearby trees. Within minutes, the horsemen left the unmoving bodies of the other women and children strewn on the ground. They galloped back into the battle, hacking and slaughtering as they went.

One lone rider saw the young woman with the bundle dive towards the bushes and pounded after her. As she crashed into the trees, Emily saw her face. *Larianna!*

She had to help her. Emily grabbed a thick stick off the ground and raced to Larianna's aid, but before she'd gone far, the man on horseback caught up to Larianna. He struck her down from behind with one blow of his claymore. She fell forward, still clutching the bundle in her arms. More men joined him, looking for other stray people, combing the edge of the bushes.

Emily had no time to feel the horror of witnessing Larianna's death. She had to save herself. She turned and ran, making it unseen deeper into the trees.

"Hey there, boy!"

Emily turned just in time to see a well-dressed warrior raise his bow and aim at her. She leapt over a fallen log and dove behind a tree, as the arrow whizzed past her and stuck into the ground scant centimetres away. She ran in spurts and then crawled on her belly into the undergrowth until she rolled into a hollow. She curled up and dragged branches over herself. As she lay quivering and holding her breath, two men beat the bushes around her.

"Leave the boy," someone ordered. "He'll starve anyway before much time has passed."

The crashing of the brush faded as the two warriors moved away. She dared not come out in case it was a trick. For many long minutes she cowered, not moving a muscle.

When at last she had decided it was safe to move, she heard a thud, then several more. She'd been right, they hadn't left her. They were pitching rocks into the trees hoping to flush her out. She had no idea how to get back to the present and save herself.

A long time passed, so much in fact that Emily felt dazed and disoriented and no longer able to tell how long she'd been in her cramped position. She strained to listen for anyone nearby, realizing all had gone strangely quiet. The silence was absolute – no bird calls, no movement of people or animals, no rustling of the wind – almost as if she had gone deaf.

Gingerly, she moved a hand, an arm, her other arm, her legs, rubbing them until she could feel blood circulating throughout her body again. Nudging away the branches covering her, she cautiously raised her head and peered about.

Only the ravages of the horrific combat were left. Bodies lay strewn across the hillside, drenched in blood.

She heaved the contents of her stomach and leaned against a tree trunk.

Picking her way back through the underbrush, she searched for Larianna. She'd become disoriented while she was being pursued and didn't know where she was. She headed for the closest way out of the thicket.

Suddenly she heard voices. Peeking through the trees, she saw several monks spread across the field, checking for life. They continued their gruesome task as several of their companions began digging a large pit.

Emily skirted the edge of the trees, keeping an eye on the monks who were all some distance from her. Although there was no hope for Larianna, she had to search for Kiresz. This was her last chance to find out what had happened to her.

Two monks headed her way and then stopped. They'd found Larianna lying just inside some trees. They shook their heads, as if signalling that she was not alive, and headed off to see to others.

Emily stumbled over to Larianna. Brushing her hair aside, she saw the face of the woman in her mirror. She bowed her head and sobbed.

She still had to find Kiresz. Had Larianna been carrying her? As tenderly as she could, Emily turned Larianna over and pulled the shawl away. There was her baby. Kiresz. A tiny, beautiful girl with her mother's oval eyes. Was she breathing?

Emily picked up the baby and listened to her chest.

She couldn't hear anything. She cleared dirt and dead leaves from her face and from inside her little mouth.

All at once, the baby let out a cry.

"Wait," Emily yelled at the disappearing figures of the monks. "Come back."

She yelled louder, until at last they heard her and the cries of the baby. Two monks rushed back.

Some excited words were exchanged, though Emily could not understand what was said. She tried to communicate the situation to them and show that she wanted them to take the baby. They seemed to recognize Larianna and her child, and finally nodded in agreement.

Emily handed the baby to one of them, who examined the infant with concern. The other took another more thorough look at Larianna, but she was gone.

He reached for the shawl and as he did so, something shifted and nestled to the ground. Both monks crossed themselves and studied the object, seeming almost afraid to pick it up.

Emily moved closer and took a sharp breath. It was the jewelled mirror! It lay on the ground, bright with reflected sun, untouched by dirt or other human hands.

With awkward movements, the monks swaddled the baby in the shawl and tucked the mirror in beside it. One set off towards the monastery, while the other picked up a shovel and began digging a hole a few metres away from the trees on a rise in a secluded spot.

"Be safe, Kiresz," Emily whispered. Then she turned once more to Larianna.

"Goodbye," she said and touched her shoulder.

Instantly, Emily was in the present.

CHAPTER SEVENTEEN

Emily stood for a few moments, stunned at the horror she'd experienced. She'd seen victims of war on television, but nothing prepared her for what being in battle was really like. There was no one she could tell, no one who would understand, except Mairead and that would have to be in a letter. Her parents would never believe her. She felt so alone.

She began to shake when she thought of how she'd nearly been killed. Sobs suddenly racked her body as she recalled the women and children who had been killed, and the poor crofters slaughtered, because they were caught in the struggles of rich and powerful men. Somehow through it all, she'd done what she had to do. She'd found Larianna and saved Kiresz.

Tears continued to course down her cheeks as she looked over the calm and beautiful hillside that once had been the scene of frenzied brutality. She'd never remember this peaceful spot without recalling the battle.

The one good thing that had emerged was that Kiresz was safe.

But did Larianna know? Mairead's words came strongly to her mind. *The mirror will give you the answers you seek.*

Emily knew exactly where to go.

She strode to the crest of the hill and into the thicket, plunging along the path through the emerald shade and into muffled silence. The moist air was thick with the scent of pine. Twigs rustled to the ground as she brushed by the low, dry branches.

When she reached the stone circle, Emily marched over to the closest flat stone and set her backpack down. She removed the carved box and balanced it on the rock. As she withdrew the mirror, the box tipped off. Emily grabbed for it, but it hit the ground before she could catch it.

She laid the mirror down in a soft bed of grass and reached for the box. The bottom seemed to have fallen out. Then she saw that there were two layers, and there was something between them.

Lifting a loose corner, she removed the first layer of thin wood from the bottom and found a folded square of thin and yellowed paper inside. She opened it and read the fine, looped handwriting.

Dear Emily,

If you are reading this, you will know that this is the note I promised to leave for you. I knew you would find this special mirror one day and that you would also know what to do with it.

Emily glanced at the signature. She smiled. Geordie, the great-uncle she had known when he was a young man, had remembered! He'd promised that if he ever found out what was hidden in the secret section under the fireplace in her grandmother's stone house he would write a note and somehow let her know. She continued to read.

I also know how curious you are and that you will not rest until you find out the answers of how it came to be yours, for it does rightfully belong to you.

Once our grandmother died, my sister Emma was to have owned it. When she, too, lost her life, Molly, your Grandmother Mary Renfrew, was next in succession. However, she never wanted or used it, and it remained in its special place, put there by our mother.

Although my mother never knew you, she did know that another descendant would come to own the mirror. I always knew it would one day be yours.

May you be led to every success in your life and use your gifts wisely, as I know you will. It has been a pleasure to know you.

Your friend and great-uncle, Geordie.

The words were swimming before her when she finished reading. Geordie's words brought so many memories back to her. Of Emma and her family and Emma's grandmother, Janet Elliott, who must have told Emma about the mirror – maybe even in her last breaths before she died.

Emily pictured Geordie tucking the note inside the box, and he and his mother hiding it under the fireplace. Replacing the folded note, Emily pieced the box back together again.

She examined the intricate markings more closely, noticing the delicate carved flowers and rosebuds. She brushed her fingers over each until she came to something she hadn't noticed on one side of the box. Initials. *GE*. Geordie must have made the box!

When she touched the initials again, she heard a soft click and a little piece on the front sprang loose, and she saw the note again. A secret compartment! She laughed. The box hadn't broken at all. Geordie loved to hide things, and he'd made a special hidden drawer in the box. Placing the box in the grass, Emily picked up the mirror.

She walked to the recumbent stone, where she'd first seen Larianna in the mist, then raised the mirror and held it quietly. When the handle warmed, Emily watched fragments of light shift and swirl in the glass. Then it once again became clear.

There was Larianna, with questioning eyes.

Emily smiled at her, and in her thoughts, guided Larianna through what she'd seen and learned. She showed Larianna images of the monk with the bundled baby in his arms, the painting of her descendant in Laird Elgivin's drawing room. Other images and conversations flashed through her mind as well, of Mairead and the visits there.

A serene joy transformed Larianna's face. She smiled a brilliant smile. and the mirror glowed.

"Thank you," Larianna whispered. *"Dewlessa."*

"Dewlessa," Emily replied, meaning it with all her heart.

A soft golden light radiated outwards, changing into shifting colours. The peaceful light flowed out and encircled Emily.

Instantly, a kaleidoscope of women's faces began appearing and dissolving in the mirror, as if each woman were introducing herself. Emily knew she was looking at all the women, for centuries back, who had owned the mirror. At least two dozen appeared, bright and clear. Their hair and clothing styles changed with the times, but their eyes all held the same loving kindness, grace and self-confidence.

Kiresz, she thought. What had happened to her?

In a flash, Emily was standing in front of the entrance to the Abbey of Deer. She saw the baby Kiresz, in the arms of a monk, being handed to a well-dressed woman with a gentle look.

"Thank you for letting us have her," the woman said. "You have answered my prayers of having a child. And her dear mother was my cousin."

The monk bowed. "I know she will be in good hands."

The woman cradled the baby with a look of joy on

her face and headed towards a man standing by a fancy carriage. He embraced them both.

So Kiresz had been adopted by a childless, well-to-do couple. Emily smiled. But how had her descendants come to be part of Laird Elgivin's family line? The surface of the glass swirled again, then cleared.

A horse-drawn carriage stood in front of a mansion with liveried servants standing on the cobblestones around it. A group of elegantly attired people stood on the sweeping steps. Emily guessed the time was somewhere within the last three hundred years, though she didn't know where it was. She was sure she'd seen the emblem on the door of the carriage before, too. But where?

In a flash, she remembered. She'd seen the same one on the top of the paper on which Mairead had written the recipe for sticky toffee pudding. Mairead must have used letterhead paper. This must be Laird Elgivin's manor house before the additions!

A young woman alighted in a white silk wedding gown with pearls at her neck. It was Kiresz from the painting! It had to be about 1808.

Now Emily realized how the mirror worked. All she had to do was think of a question and the answer appeared in images she could see as clearly as if she were there.

She tried it again. How had the mirror come into her family?

Just as swiftly, Emily was seeing the wide steps of a

stone house, looking down at lawns with beds of wild-flowers, and the occasional treed nook that stretched down to a gazebo in plain sight, its base rimmed with small shoots of ivy and low bushes of pink eglantine roses.

A small, dark-haired girl and a young boy raced down the gravel paths, chasing each other and giggling.

Emily turned and looked at the house. She was at the back entrance to Murdoch's home. She could see the library through the French doors.

The doors opened and Kiresz came out.

"Emmarie, stop running and come in, please," she called. "Jack, your mum is waiting with your dinner in the kitchen."

Emily turned back to the children playing tag. As they ran past her, she caught a better look at the young girl. It was definitely the daughter from the painting!

As the boy rounded the corner of the house to the kitchen door, the girl climbed the steps and took her mother's hand.

"Mama, why cannot Jack eat with us?"

"I've told you before, quinie, he is the son of our cook and gardener, and he must not eat with the family in the dining room when your father has guests."

"I don't care about Papa's guests. I'd rather have a picnic with Jack."

"Soon, my darling." Kiresz gave her daughter a hug and they disappeared through the French doors.

A shimmer of light passed before Emily's eyes. She

saw that the flowers and trees had grown, the paths were grassy, and she knew time had shifted again. The eglantine rose bushes, high and lush with blossoms, set off the ivy that grew halfway up the gazebo, and she heard voices coming from it. She moved closer so she could see inside.

Emmarie was now a lovely young woman. "Oh, Jack, yes."

"But will your father agree? You'll be plain Mrs. Robertson instead of a great lady." Jack was now a sturdy young man.

"Don't worry. Mama will take our side, and he'll come around."

"Emmarie," Jack said, "I hope we have at least two daughters. Kiresz for your mother, and Mairead for mine."

"What if we have all boys?" Emmarie teased.

"Oh no," Jack said. "I'm sure we'll have two daughters."

They stepped out of the gazebo and headed back towards the house, arm in arm.

Now Emily had the answer to her last remaining questions. Emmarie Lowry and Jack Robertson were the link to the Elliott family – and to Murdoch's. She also suspected Jack's mother was the ancestor of Mairead, Murdoch's housekeeper. They were all related to each other, though the links spread farther apart down the generations.

More images flashed through the mirror. Women, children, families and weddings – some elegant and refined, others obviously poorer; some happy, some sad. Names came to mind, each blending with the next. It wasn't necessary or even possible to memorize them all – Emily knew in her heart that she'd be able to recall the women in a moment. If she ever needed them, they were all there for her, too; she only had to look in the mirror.

Emily knew that she had come from a strong circle of women, who had endured hard obstacles and demanding conditions in their lives. They had all done their best through being independent and honourable, and behaving with dignity and love.

As the images in the mirror came closer to Emily's own time, she saw her great-aunt Emma and Grandmother Renfrew smiling at her and knew they would always be with her. They were part of the circle of magic within the mirror, and so was she.

Emily looked over the valleys to Scroghill Farm and the stone house with its two chimneys. She thought of the lives her Elliott ancestors had led there, and of their struggles to re-establish themselves in a new country. From Larianna and Kiresz to Emma and Grandmother Renfrew, she was proud to be part of this gifted family line.

But there were other female ancestors too, equally important – the women like Mairead, the keepers of the mirror's legend.

Emily thought of her own mother, and how strong and independent she was. Kate was like Larianna in her fierce concern for her child's well-being. Larianna tried to keep her child safe during a terrible war. Kate did the same through her struggles as a self-reliant career mom.

Emily replaced the mirror in the carved box, satisfied for the moment. When she needed to know more, all she had to do was consult the mirror.

She caught sight of her dad, making his way towards her.

Surprisingly, Emily realized she didn't need him as much anymore, at least not in the same way. Her parents were two people with different goals in life and different ways of achieving them. It wasn't her fault that they'd split up, nor could anything she did or said bring them back together.

There was also nothing she could do about either of them working all the time, except perhaps reminding them to take it easy from time to time. None of that meant they didn't love her.

Emily knew that her dad cared for her very deeply. Even though her parents might never get back together, he was still her dad and always would be. They might not have the special times together anymore as a family, but she and her dad would create more, just as she and her mother would. She had a role to fill as their daughter, and one day she would get married and have her own children – well, two daughters, according to Mairead – and pass the mirror on to one of them.

Her dad could only be who he was. He couldn't be everything she wanted him to be. No one could. She couldn't be the perfect daughter either. She blushed, thinking about all the complaining she'd done, even though some of it hadn't been spoken out loud. At least Dad tried sometimes. He'd taken her where she'd wanted to go, when he felt able. Maybe if she'd let him have a few hours to himself each day, he wouldn't have been so tired.

Dad walked up and Emily hugged him hard.

"Don't you have work to do?" she asked. "Maybe if we go back right away you could get it done before we leave for your geological dig tomorrow. I could use a little time out from sightseeing, so I'll be ready for hiking up Ben Nevis and exploring that national geological park you wanted to see."

Dad raised his eyebrows and shook his head in wonder.

"Let's shake a leg, then," he said with a smile.

She smiled broadly.

Maybe there wasn't much left of the old way Dad used to be – except his corny sayings – but she wasn't the same daughter either. So what if things were a little awkward right now, as they found their new way? She saw the love reflected in his eyes.

Dad was taking a last look at the massive stones of Aikey Brae circle.

Emily stepped into the middle of the standing stones. She let her mind drift, and the breeze wash over her.

She wasn't surprised when a gentle mist appeared and she was transported back in time again. The mist cleared, and she gazed over the stone circle without any trees to obstruct the view, turning to take in all the views.

Down the north hillside, she saw a glint of light where the sun glared off something white. It was the place where she'd seen the monk the day she visited the Abbey of Deer. This was where Larianna had fallen on the day of the battle, and where she was buried.

The monk spoke a prayer over her grave, then carried his bundle of sticks down the hill. As he moved aside, the hair on the back of Emily's neck stood on end.

Now there was only one white cross!

Had she changed history by finding Kiresz and helping the monks save her that day on the battlefield? Was that why she had to bring the mirror back? She couldn't imagine how that could be possible, but she didn't know how else to explain it.

She cleared her mind again and gazed down the north slope of Aikey Brae. She thought of all that had happened there, of lives lived and lost, shaped and changed. Now she was part of that history.

In that moment, the scene disappeared, and Dad was waving her over.

Taking one final look over the stone circle, Emily swung the backpack onto her shoulders, ready to move forward into her future.

ACKNOWLEDGEMENTS

Thanks to my son, Aaron, and my parents, Stan and Elaine Iles, for travelling with me to Scotland and for accommodating me while I did research for this book: tromping through cemeteries and fields, visiting local history centres, museums and historical spots, and stopping the car on a moment's notice any time I wanted a photograph.

Thank you to Charlie Morrison for setting me on the right track when I first started my research in Maud and who kept me there. I raise a pint to you! Very special thanks to Oliver and Margaret Fuller, who helped me immensely while I was in Maud and indulged my every request as we traipsed about the surrounding countryside. Oliver, your assistance, was beyond my every expectation and I am in your debt!

Thank you to all the wonderful people I met in Maud and for everyone's assistance, large and small. I hope all the residents of Maud will forgive my fictional rearrangement and additions to their village and the surrounding area.

Thanks to my dedicated, diligent and delightful editor, Barbara Sapergia, for guiding the transformation of this book into its satisfying and rewarding conclusion.

And one final thank you to John Shaw for the personal research he did on behalf of my ancestors, who once lived at Scroghill, and which I was able to incorporate into this story.

ABOUT THE AUTHOR

JUDITH SILVERTHORNE is a multiple-award-winning author from Regina, Saskatchewan, Canada with nine books to her credit, including seven children's novels and two adult non-fiction works. She has also written several hundred articles for newspapers and magazines, and has worked as a researcher, and television documentary producer. She has presented hundreds of readings and writing workshops at libraries, schools and other educational institutions, and at conferences. She is an avid traveller, although she has spent most of her life in Saskatchewan where most of her stories are set.

www.judithsilverthorne.ca

Printed and bound in Canada by Friesens